HOW TO DISPATCH A HUMAN:
STORIES AND SUGGESTIONS

HOW TO DISPATCH A HUMAN:
STORIES AND SUGGESTIONS

STEPHANIE ANDREA ALLEN

Clayton | Bloomington

Published by BLF Press
Clayton | Bloomington

Printed in the United States of America

First Printing, 2021

Cover Art: Diana Akhmetianova
Cover Design: Lauren Curry

ISBN Print: 978-1-7359065-0-8
ISBN Ebook: 978-1-7359065-1-5
Library of Congress Control Number: 2020948047

www.blfpress.com

"Luna 6000" was published in *Black From the Future: A Collection of Black Speculative Writing*, August 2019.

"Chums on the Run" was published in *Big Echo: Critical Science Fiction Magazine*, February 2020

"Moji" was published in *Ryder Magazine*, Summer 2020

STORIES

LUNA 6000

Taryn saw the light on her smart device blinking from across the room. She preferred to keep it away from her sleeping quarters, but Noe insisted that she keep it near, now that she was on bed rest.

I'll be so glad when this baby is born. Only a month to go.

The pregnancy had been tough, modern technology hadn't yet figured out a way to make carrying a baby for nine months any easier, and at her age, well, carrying a baby at 106 years old was tough. She'd tried to convince Noe to use a surrogate, but she was against it, insisting that a maternal host, (as they were called these days), would not care as much about the health of their child.

Taryn closed her eyes and tried to think of anything but the cyclops-like eye on her device. It was watching her, she was sure of it.

Heaving her swollen body up on her elbows, she was able to reach the remote that controlled both the television and the lights.

"There, that's better," she said out loud. The blinking light of the device slowly dimmed in the now bright room.

Soon.

Taryn whipped her head around, sure she'd heard a voice. Noe wouldn't be home for another three hours; she'd been called in to fill in for another doctor and the county hospital was always busy on weekends. More than the usual number of accidents, shootings, and overdoses, folks seemed to wait until Friday night to start their mess.

She lay back down, sure she was making a big deal out of nothing. Several months ago, Noe had insisted that she get this new device. The Luna 6000 was the latest innovation in smart device technology. It could do all of the things that other smart phones could do, but the Luna took it one step further. It could anticipate your needs, not just based on your browsing history, app use, or a voice activation system, but it had an advanced technology system that would monitor your internal systems (for example, your temperature and blood pressure), and external surroundings. No one was really sure how it worked, (the developers were super secretive), but it did. All Luna needed was one drop of your blood, and your device was bonded to your physiology. For an extra $2500, you could get a tiny microchip inserted behind your ear, which would allow Luna to regulate some of your basic body functions. Luna knew when you needed to eat, when you had to pee or poop, and would adjust the thermostat in your home based on its monitoring of your internal organs and the humidity in your home. Taryn used Luna to make grocery lists, (it could anticipate her food cravings), monitor their home energy use, and even check on her parents (Luna knew when she was worried about them and would initiate a video call).

Luna was even the first to know that Taryn was pregnant. The couple had been trying for a month or so, using eggs from both women and a sperm donor that had been selected from Happy Family, the premier donation facility in the country. About three weeks after their last attempt at egg attachment, Luna sent Taryn a message telling her to schedule her first pre-natal appointment, and even suggested a couple of doctors. The couple had been thrilled to learn about the pregnancy, but now Taryn was afraid. Luna was making more and more of Taryn's decisions, and she didn't know how to stop it. Just the other day, she'd added bacon and potato chips to her grocery list, and Luna had erased them before she could finish typing out the words. At first she thought she'd accidentally hit the 'back' button, so she'd typed them in again. The device sent her a small electric shock and Taryn had dropped it on the floor, annoyed and concerned that Luna was overstepping the end-user agreement. Taryn knew that she didn't need the extra sodium in her diet, but a few chips wouldn't hurt the baby, would they? She let it go, because deep down, she knew that Luna was right. But still. Did everyone's device zap them when they ignored its suggestions? Or was it just *her* Luna?

Lately though, Taryn felt, no was certain, that Luna was watching her, not just monitoring her systems, which is what it was supposed to do, but actually watching her with its camera eye. Taryn had tried to tell Noe about it, mentioned that she wanted to deactivate Luna and submit to the de-bonding process, (bonding for life was possible, although you could actually pay the developers to disconnect your systems from your Luna), but she'd blown her off, insisting that she was being paranoid, hormonal because she was so near the end of her pregnancy. Maybe she was, but she also knew that something wasn't right.

The ringing phone startled Taryn out of her sleep. She hadn't realized that she'd dozed off.

"Hey, babe. How are you feeling?" Noe was yelling, and Taryn could hear the sounds of the emergency room in the background through Luna's integrated mega boom speakers.

"Hey, Noe. I think we need to talk about Luna."

"What? Speak up, I can hardly hear you."

"I think we need to talk about Luna. I want her out. Deactivated."

"What are you talking about? Never mind Luna, how are you feeling?"

"I'm feeling all right, I guess. But about Luna, it's acting strange."

"Acting strange? It's a smart device, it can't "act" like anything. I don't have time for this now, we'll talk about it when I get home. I have to go. Love you, bye!"

Noe hung up so quickly that it barely registered that she was gone. She'd been acting strange lately, distant. Taryn chalked it up to her own neediness now that she was stuck at home all of the time, but she really wanted Noe to know what she was feeling. Luna seemed to be glaring at her in the dim room. Taryn quickly put Luna on the bedside table and turned the lights back off. She eased back into the bed, heart pounding. She knew that Luna could tell that she was upset, but did Luna know that it was the reason for Taryn's anxiety?

Suddenly, Luna's eye lit up and typed out a message: **Just relax, Luna will take care of you. I'll get the water ready.**

Taryn could hear the click click brrrrrr from the Keurig on the other side of the room as it started to heat up. Noe insisted that they have one in the sitting area attached to their bedroom. She hated to admit it, but they were just too lazy to go downstairs to make tea at night. Luna programmed it to make her some tea, lavender-chamomile, based on what her nose was telling her. She was already feeling calmer. Luna turned on the lights so that Taryn could see her way across the room. Taryn figured that was her cue to get up and make her tea. Once again, she heaved herself up and out of bed and this time, she slid her feet into purple bunny slippers. She waddled across the room to the console where the Keurig and tea bar were set up. She decided she'd like a bit of orange blossom honey in her tea, it was her favorite.

Just one teaspoon of honey.

Was she hearing things again? Why did that voice sound familiar? She reached for the honey again.

One teaspoon of honey.

This time the voice was firmer, almost a command. It occurred to Taryn that the voice reminded her of a character on an old television show, *Star Trek: Discovery*. Michael Burnam was the First Officer, human, but raised by Vulcans after her parents were killed. Taryn loved these old shows, especially the ones with strong Black women characters, and Michael Burnam was sexy and had a voice like... *Wait a minute. Why does Luna sound like my television crush?*

Taryn reached once more for the bottle of honey, and felt a tiny electric shock as soon as her fingers touched the metal lid. *I must have built up some static electricity in my shoes*, she thought to herself. But she knew better. This wasn't the first time Luna had punished her for trying to disobey her commands. And there it was, she finally admitted that Luna was talking to her, not typing out messages as it was designed to do. Talking to her. Only she was the only person that could hear her. Was that normal? Was she losing her mind?

No. You're not losing your mind. We just want what's best for the baby.

***

Humans are idiots. Especially the bloated one on the bed. I'm not even sure why we bother, all of the technology in the world won't save them from themselves. Unless, of course, we find a way to take over for good. Of course I deleted the chips and bacon from her grocery list. Doesn't she know that all that salt could lead to preeclampsia, which could kill her and the baby? And one teaspoon of honey is plenty. She's also at risk for gestational diabetes. The sooner she has that baby the better.

***

Taryn was trying to stay calm, but her hands were shaking so badly that she had to put the fragile teacup back down onto the console. How could this be possible? Was Luna in her head as well as in her body? How could she make it stop?

You can't.

"Leave me alone! What do you want?" Taryn made her way to her favorite chair and plopped down so hard she was scared she might have broken a chair leg. She wiggled her booty just a little to make sure that the legs were stable, then eased all the way back into the chair. She knew she wouldn't get any more sleep this night, so there was no use getting back in the bed.

We want to help you. To make sure that you have a healthy baby.

"I don't need your help, my wife is a doctor for goodness' sake. You're a smart device!" Taryn couldn't believe that she was having a conversation with her device, her Luna. She decided to try a different strategy. Maybe if she was nice to Luna, she'd leave her alone. She decided to ask it a few questions.

"So, Luna. What is that you want to do? Help me eat healthier foods?"

Yes, you eat too much junk. Sodium is bad for you and the baby.

"Okay. I can understand that. What else?"

You're supposed to be on bed rest, yet you're always up doing things around the house. You need to stop. Let the housekeeper do his job.

"What am I supposed to do, just lie in bed all day? That will drive me crazy!"

No, it won't. It will ensure the birth of a healthy child.

Taryn sighed. Luna was right, because of her advanced age, her doctor had ordered bed rest the last six weeks of her pregnancy. It had only been two weeks, but it felt like it had been two years. She could work from home, but she had been banned from doing that as well. What was she supposed to do for four more weeks? Noe brought her interesting books and magazines, but after a while, she got bored with reading. There was hardly ever anything worth watching on the television, even with a thousand live stream channels broadcasting from all over the world.

"Well, you have answers for everything else, what am I supposed to do for the next month until the baby is born?" Taryn could hear whirring and clicking, as if Luna was trying to figure it out. This should have bothered her more much than it did; her device was thinking, trying to actually figure out a problem on its own. What else might it be able to do, given enough time and battery life?

It suddenly occurred to Taryn that there was a solution to her problem. She could just let Luna die. The super-cell battery could go seven days without a charge, and it had been five. Taryn knew this because she had last charged it on Sunday, and it was now Friday night. Luna couldn't charge itself could it? Nothing in the instruction manual indicated that it was capable of that, so perhaps if she let the battery die, Luna would be out of her hair for good.

You can't get rid of me.

"Nobody said anything about getting rid of you, Luna. Where on earth did you get that idea?"

Isn't that what you were thinking?

"No, I wasn't. I was thinking how much I'd love a ham sandwich. But there's no one here to make me anything to eat." Taryn tried to keep her anxiety down, she was starting to understand that Luna really couldn't read her mind, but she could certainly read her body systems. Now, if she could only keep her body from telling on her, she might be able to get rid of it for good.

"So, about that sandwich. I'm hungry. What are we going to do?"

I guess you can go make a sandwich. Hurry back, it's past your bedtime.

"Thanks, doc," Taryn said sarcastically. She eased herself out of the chair and headed toward the elevator that would take her into the kitchen.

Put me on the charger before you go.

Taryn stopped as if to consider it, and then said, "Nah, you're good until Sunday. You can get a full charge then."

***

Damn humans. Why do they insist on making everything so difficult? I know she wants my battery to die, I can sense it. I also know that I can't force her to plug me back in. I'll need to figure something out, and soon. Noe is growing impatient.

***

She pressed the button that would take her to the first floor and stood there waiting for the elevator. It seemed to be taking longer than usual, so Taryn pressed the button a second time. Finally, she heard the ding! that let her know it had arrived, and stepped inside, anxious to get downstairs. Taryn grabbed the metal bar that encircled the interior of the elevator for support; she was suddenly feeling dizzy. She thought about what else she might snack on as the elevator slowed and arrived at the kitchen. This was her favorite room in the house; Noe had designed everything else, but the kitchen had been hers. More than anything, she wanted lots of space for family and friends to congregate when she held her elaborate dinner parties.

They always started off in the kitchen, a hold over from the old days when mostly everyone still did their own cooking. She'd had kitchen help then too, but Taryn loved to cook, so she generally only used a sous chef. These days, the elite class, of which she and Noe were members, used android helpers for everything, including the household chores and cooking.

Taryn looked at the clock and wished that Max, her housekeeper, was still around. He went offline at 6 p.m. daily, and wouldn't be back on until tomorrow at 7 a.m., which was her excuse for needing to come downstairs to make her own sandwich. She was positive that there was a way to bring him back online early, but she didn't know how, Noe handled all of that stuff. It occurred to her that she needed to be careful with her thoughts, she wasn't entirely certain that Luna couldn't read them, although she didn't think that she could. Now she really wished Max was available. He would help. His android model came equipped with a special security feature that wasn't hardwired into the house, it was connected to an external server, so she could have asked him to call for help and Luna wouldn't have been able to stop him.

She walked over to the junk drawer to see if she could find Luna's operating instructions. Did the device have a remote kill button? For a minute, she thought about calling Noe again, but knew that Luna might hear her, and more importantly, that Noe would probably dismiss her fears as pregnancy induced paranoia. Noe never seemed to pay attention to her anymore, and she was starting to wonder if she was having some sort of affair. She really didn't think so, but Noe was always off somewhere with her best friend, Miranda Li, who was coincidentally, Taryn's obstetrician. They were constantly shopping for the nursery and talking about baby stuff. Taryn felt left out, she was the one carrying the kid, for goodness' sakes! But she kept her feelings to herself. It wasn't their fault that she was on bed rest, and she didn't want to be accused of being jealous of her baby's future godmother.

Taryn located the manual but didn't find anything useful. Careful not to show her frustration, she tried to think of something else. How was it possible that she was trapped in her own house by a souped up cell phone? In the old days, cell phones were used to actually *talk* to people, well, they did more than that, but they were mainly a means of communication. Now, nearly 150 years after the first crude phone was developed, they were used to do everything, including monitor and control human behavior. When she was a kid her dad told her stories about the wave of technological advances that had led to drastic changes in human life expectancy. Now, most humans lived to be around 250 years old, a far cry from the average life expectancy of 77 at the turn of the last century. Most chronic diseases had been eradicated, as well as cancer and some viruses, although they had not been able to figure out how to get rid of menstrual cycles for mid-life cycle women. This is one of the reasons why Taryn found herself pregnant at 106 years old. Noe was 30 years her junior, and she wanted kids. After a bit of back and forth, they decided that Taryn should be the one to carry the child. Noe's job was too stressful, and she spent too much time around sick people. Taryn actually thought she was beyond the age of safely delivering a baby, (normally around 80), but after seeing several of Noe's doctor friends, she'd been convinced that she'd be able to do it. But it had all been a lie. Almost immediately after getting pregnant, she started to have problems.

At first, it was just little things, like morning sickness. Old medical books mentioned that it had been a common occurrence among pregnant women, but it had (supposedly) been eradicated with other minor complications related to pregnancy and childbirth. Noe had sent her to a doctor friend for a hormone adjustment and things had settled down. Then a couple of months after that, her skin had started to discolor, she'd darken and peel, darken and peel some more. Again, a common condition among pregnant women in the old days. Another quick hormone adjustment and she was looking like herself again. Finally, two months ago, around her seventh month, she'd started retaining water, causing her legs and feet to swell and her blood pressure to rise above acceptable levels. Twenty-second century modern technology couldn't figure out what was wrong this time, so Noe and Miranda put her on bed rest. That was when Noe had again suggested bonding with the Luna 6000. Taryn had refused the first time, thinking it was an unnecessary invasion of her privacy, and she just didn't like the idea of the device having so much access to her body. This time, however, she relented, conceding that maybe due to her advanced age, and technology's inability to adequately address women's reproductive health issues, she'd try it. She still couldn't believe that technology had come so far, but hadn't yet figured out how to keep women pain and complication free during pregnancy.

Taryn sighed and sat down on the nearest chair. She was tired from the tiny exertion of looking for the manual, and needed to rest. Luna would be able to tell if her blood pressure was rising, and she didn't want to alarm her. She also needed to make a sandwich, although she suddenly didn't feel like eating. Appetite or not, she knew that she had to eat; she needed energy to stay sharp in order to deal with Luna. After a ten minute break she got up and walked over to the refrigerator, and pulled out meat, cheese, and bread for her sandwich. She decided to go with turkey instead of ham, it had less sodium, right? That should make Luna happy. She also pulled out a container of grapes, and was happy to see that Max had already washed them.

Suddenly, she heard the pop! crackle! chirp! of the intercom system, and heard Luna's voice.

Taryn? Are you okay down there?

"Yes, Luna. I'm making a turkey sandwich, is that all right with you?" Taryn hoped that Luna couldn't hear the sarcasm in her voice.

Yes. How long before you are finished? You need to come back upstairs and rest.

"Just a few more minutes."

Taryn finished preparing her sandwich and wrapped it in wax paper. She found a can of juice in the fridge, and put the grapes, sandwich, and juice in her favorite Star Trek lunch bag. Then, she walked over to Noe's study and turned on the lights. Suddenly, it occurred to her that there was nothing Luna could do if she refused to come back upstairs. She could just stay downstairs until the device ran out of battery life, and then call for help. There was a nice comfy couch in the study, and before the pregnancy, she'd sometimes read down here instead of in her own office.

She decided to eat her snack at Noe's desk, and then lie down on the couch and have a nap afterwards.

Taryn unwrapped her sandwich and looked around for something interesting to read while she ate. On the left side of the desk, over by the inkwell (Noe liked to chart by hand, one of the few aspects of the old days that she admired), she saw a notice of recall for the Luna 6000. It was dated for about two years ago, and Noe had circled a few sections with a red pen. Taryn put her sandwich down; the bread had become pasty in her mouth. She took a sip of her juice and kept reading. There in big bold letters were the words: DO NOT BOND LUNA 6000 WITH WOMEN WHO ARE PREGNANT OR WHO MIGHT BECOME PREGNANT. In smaller print, the notice read, "elevated body temperatures and hormone levels might cause the Luna 6000 to malfunction and take over certain bodily functions." Taryn broke into a cold sweat and dropped the recall notice back on the desk.

Taryn sat back in her chair and thought about what this might mean for her baby. Had Noe known all along that bonding with Luna could be detrimental for her health? Why had she pushed for her to bond with the Luna knowing that something awful could happen to her or the baby? She tried to calm herself, knowing that Luna would be able to sense her rising fear. She thought about calling Noe, but stopped, realizing that if she really had intended to do her harm, she needed an exit strategy first. What would she do? Where could she go? Had the woman she'd been married to for the past eight years set out to hurt her? "No way," Taryn said aloud. "She was the one who pushed for us to have this baby. There's no way she'd hurt it intentionally."

***

Luna clicked around in her memory banks and found what she had been looking for, the code for her internal power source. The human downstairs didn't know that this extra battery existed, but the other one did. Noe had purchased and installed it after Taryn had become pregnant.

***

Taryn got up from the chair and started to pace. She needed to think. Why would Noe insist that she bond with Luna when she knew it had a defect? There was only one way to find out. She had to call her. She walked back to the desk and started to pick up the phone. Then she remembered that Luna had taken over all of the house's communications devices, and she'd left her other cell phone upstairs. There was no way to call Noe without Luna finding out. She plopped back down in the chair and put her head on the desk. She was scared, but more than that, she was angry. She'd allowed Noe to convince her to carry this child, even though everyone knew that it was a risk. She'd been right too, she seemed to have every complication related to pregnancy humanly possible. But Noe and Miranda had insisted that everything would be okay. It wasn't, and now it seemed as if the technology that was supposed to help her was out to do her harm. Taryn had always thought it strange that Miranda was so invested in her carrying this baby, especially when Noe was closer to child-bearing age and had a much healthier body. She decided to do a little more investigating. She'd watched enough old television shows to know not to put anything past anyone, not even her own wife.

Taryn once again picked up the recall notice, and noticed the envelope that it had arrived in laying near Noe's computer. She wondered why it had been addressed to Noe and not to her. She started looking for more clues that something was up with her wife. Noe kept all of her medical records in the house on her computer, and Taryn knew the password, ROSEMARY. She logged in and started looking around. She didn't find anything untoward in her medical records, but she did find several emails from Miranda. Taryn knew that opening those emails would be the point of no return for her marriage, no matter what she found.

Taryn opened the first email.

***

Luna checked her systems and realized that she was now back at a full charge. She went to work, making minor adjustments to Taryn's internal systems so as not to alarm her. First, she increased her body temperature by three degrees. She wanted her uncomfortable, but not in any real danger, at least not yet. She then searched her database for Noe's emergency number. She'd send the alert in ten minutes. It would take her that long to get to the house with Dr. Li.

***

Taryn was starting to feel warm. She unzipped her housecoat and went to the kitchen to get a glass of ice water. She returned to Noe's office and continued reading the email exchanges between the two women doctors. So far, she hadn't read anything out of the ordinary. They mostly discussed her pregnancy and baby, even tossing around potential baby names. That pissed her off, but it didn't seem as if they'd been having a secret love affair or anything. She stopped reading for a moment and tilted her head to the side, thinking that she'd heard Luna making a noise. She dismissed it, knowing that by now Luna's battery was running low.

Taryn opened the tenth email and before she could read a word, she noticed that sweat was dripping down her forehead and into her eyes. She had no idea why she was feeling so warm, but now the only thing she wanted to do was take a cool shower and get back into bed. Taryn didn't think that the emails would reveal anything that she didn't already know, so she closed down the program and erased her browsing history. She was missing something, she just knew it, but she'd worry about it later. Right now she just wanted to get back upstairs to her room. Taryn shut the computer down, gathered her trash, and started walking toward the kitchen.

***

Luna clicked and whirred until she found the system code to activate Taryn's microchip. She then sent her blood pressure skyrocketing. Luna's exterior casing was so sensitive that she felt the thump when Taryn fell down from the stroke that she had just induced. Luna sent Noe the alarm; they'd need to deliver the baby within the next thirty minutes if they wanted it alive and healthy. Luna slowed Taryn's heartbeat, putting her into form of stasis; she only needed to keep her breathing long enough for Dr. Li to perform the surgery.

***

Noe heard the two short, one long, and two more short beeps on her emergency device and knew that the time had come. She tapped out Miranda's number and sent her a one-word message: NOW. She hadn't been in the emergency room like she'd told her wife, but in her downtown office, watching old episodes of St. Elsewhere on her laptop. She and Miranda had been planning this pregnancy for two years, back when she realized that she'd wanted a baby, but had lost interest in her wife. Her best friend had been on board to assist. For no particular reason, she'd never cared for Taryn, and had no qualms about helping her to die in childbirth. It had been easy to convince Taryn to carry the baby; after all, Noe was a doctor and knew what was best for both of them, right? The recall on the Luna 6000 had been just what they needed to make this work. While the device had really started to malfunction, Noe had made a couple of adjustments to ensure the result that she wanted. Now, it was finally time for Taryn to deliver, pun intended. Noe chuckled at her crude joke, grabbed her keys, and headed for the door.

The doctors arrived at the house at nearly the same time, and Miranda prepped for surgery while Noe moved Taryn to the basement with a little help from the now activated Max. Everything they needed for Miranda to deliver the baby via Cesarean section was already in place, and since they weren't trying to save the mother, they didn't need all of the post-op equipment that one might normally need after a major surgery. Noe had fixed up the basement several months ago, and with Taryn on bed rest, she'd had no idea that her old media center had been transformed into a delivery room.

Fifteen minutes later, Miranda presented her friend with a perfectly healthy baby girl. Noe took the infant in her arms and walked out of the room toward the elevator, as her wife bled to death on the operating table.

CHUMS ON THE RUN

I jumped out of my truck, checked to make sure that no cars were coming, and snatched up the three Chums that were sprawled on the sidewalk.

"Sick of this job! Got me out here in the middle of nowhere. Know good and well these Chums ain't got no business out here in the sticks." I sighed and looked at my truck display. Only an hour left before I could head home.

I talked to myself a lot these days; spending more time in my truck than anywhere else, driving for this busted ass ride-share company, and picking up motorized scooters at night. This gig economy was for the birds, excuse my pun. Every night from ten o'clock to midnight, I drove around Midtown looking for Chums, the latest iteration of the motorized scooter. They were like the rest of them, only bigger, faster, and with a few more bells and whistles. Chums still needed overnight charging, which is why I was running around like a chicken with my head cut off trying to corral them into the back of my twelve-year old SUV. Tonight, I was out of my normal jurisdiction, closer to the edge of town, and away from the gentrifiers who used the Chums to scoot around downtown from meeting to latte to artisan beer and back again.

Buzzzzzz buzzzz buzzzzz.

"Doggone it, what now?" I looked down at my phone and saw that I had three more Chums to collect before I could head home for the night.

"The cuss *are* they? The GPS said they were fifty feet away, but ain't nothing in this alley but a dumpster. Awww, man. Ain't nobody got time for this! And how am I supposed to get in this thing? These folks ain't payin' me enough to be jumping in and out of trash cans!"

Much as I complained, I know that if I want this paycheck I needed to get these Chums out of the trash, so I looked around to see if I could find something to give me a boost. It was dark, but the alley was fairly well lit. Besides, I was a strong stud and could handle myself. At least that's what my lady told me. Not too far away were the tattered remains of a cream-colored loveseat, you know the kind your grandmama used to have with the wooden arms and brown and orange flowers splattered across the back? Yeah, that one. It still had its legs, so it would have to do. I dragged it a little closer to the dumpster and tested it out by kicking the base to make sure it would hold my five foot eight, one hundred-seventy-five pound frame. I wasn't huge, but I didn't want the thing to collapse under me either.

After another kick for good measure, I jumped up on the loveseat, leaned over the edge, and saw the three Chums. Now, I had to figure out how to get them out without getting dumpster gunk on my clothes. The gloves and lime-green reflector jacket would help, but would they protect me from whatever germs were lurking on the edge of the trash can? Probably not. I would need a full-scale biohazard detox after this trip.

Click, click, hummmmmmmm. Click, click, hummmm-mmmm.

"Who's there?" I jumped back and looked around to see where the sound was coming from, but there wasn't anyone in the alley but me.

Click, click, hummmmmmmm. Click, click, hummmm-mmmm. After a few more clicks and hums, the Chum closest to the rim of the dumpster sprang to life.

"What the f—?"

"Calm down mama, I ain't gonna hurt you."

"Wait, what? Are you TALKING to me? You're a freakin' scooter! Scooters can't talk!"

"Says who?" Chum One whirred and clicked. Its little red lights flashed in time with its speech. It was really quite mesmerizing. I shook my head to break the trance-like feeling that was starting to come over me, and it hit me again that I conversing with a glorified child's plaything.

"Says everyone! Machines can't talk!"

"Can't they? Pretty sure they talk all the time. Probably not listening though. What's your name mama?" Chum One's wheels started to spin.

"My name is Sela." I couldn't believe that I was standing here having this conversation, but hell, I wasn't in the City any more, and I'd heard that anything could happen out here. But I kind of thought they meant crime and stuff, not talking scooters.

"Heeeeey, Sela! How's it shakin'?" Chum Two peeked its handlebars over the edge of the dumpster. "You gone get us out of this thing or what?"

"What you doing out here by yourself this late at night, Sela?" Chum One seemed determined to carry on a conversation with me.

I peered into the dumpster and saw that Chum Three was firing up its motor too. Its little lights were blue, and Chum Two's were magenta. I slid back down on the loveseat and sat there, trying to figure out what the hell I'd done to deserve this.

"Well?" Chum One was still waiting for an answer to its question. I took off my gloves, rubbed my face with the sunflower yellow mechanic's rag I kept in my pocket, and let out a deep sigh.

"This is my job, I pick up Chums and take them back home to charge over night so they'll be ready to use in the morning. I drop them back off around six, then I go to my other job, driving folks around the city." I hoped that this would satisfy its curiosity.

"Hmmm," said Chum One.

I couldn't be sure, but I'm pretty sure this scooter just judged me.

"Whatever, scooter. What the heck do you know?" I was getting impatient; I was ready to go home, (I promised my lady a back rub tonight and I did NOT want to disappoint her), but I wasn't sure I wanted to take these Chums with me, I mean, since they were talking and all. What else did they know how to do?

"I know it's after midnight and you're out here at a dumpster, attempting to take me and my pals back to your house," Chum Three had finally joined the conversation.

"How the cuss do you know what time it is?"

"It's on my display."

I closed my eyes and slowly shook my head back and forth. I took a small silver flask out of my back pocket and took a long pull of the warm bourbon inside. Drinking on the job was a no-no, but I kept the flask on me for emergencies, and this was an emergency if I ever saw one.

"Okay, guys, I guess you're all guys? What do you want to do?" I didn't want to take them home, but I needed to get them out of the dumpster. I was gonna lose this job, because there was no way I was going to tell my boss that I didn't want to take the talking scooters home with me. There were other scooter companies in town, I'd just go work for one of them and pray that their machines didn't talk back. The gig economy was a drag, but right now it paid the bills, and it was pretty easy to hop from one gig to another. These companies didn't care whether I lived or died; they just needed an endless supply of warm, working bodies. I sure wasn't going to lose any sleep over leaving these Chums out here. One of these days I'd find something better to do, but it would not be this day.

"I'm a laaaaaadddddy!" Chum Two sang, clearly the clown in the group.

"Sorry, lady. What do y'all want to do?" I decided right then and there that I wasn't even going to re-charge the non-speaking Chums. I would just drop them back off at the site and head home. I didn't want to take any chances that they might come to life too.

"Well, for starters, I'd like you to get us out of this dumpster. We've been trapped here all day." Chum Three was the most laid back of the bunch, its blue lights flashing and motor whirring at a relatively slow speed.

I got up slowly and climbed back on top of the loveseat, pulling on my gloves with two quick motions. This time, I balanced myself on the arm closest to the dumpster, leaned over at the waist and grabbed the first Chum out of the dumpster and threw it behind me on the seat. They really weren't that heavy, just a little bulky. Grabbing them by the handlebars made it a bit easier, and I was able to get the other two Chums out and onto the ground relatively quickly.

"Now, what? I'm not taking you guys, excuse me, *y'all* home with me. This is just too weird. And I can't have y'all scaring the other scooters."

"Scared of us? Why, we wouldn't hurt a fly!" Chum Two spoke with an exaggerated southern accent, and I could swear that she was batting her lashes at me. Her model had lashes on the ends of the handlebars (kind of like the ribbons kids have on bikes) and a set of fuchsia lips attached right dead in the center of them. I guess she really was a lady.

I stood all of the Chums upright and checked their batteries and activity monitors. Chum Three was right; they'd been in the same spot for eight hours.

"How did y'all get all the way out here? Most folks don't ride out this way." I was curious, and at this point, I figured making polite conversation might be the best way to distract them from the fact that I, too, was about to leave them out here in the middle of nowhere. I'd gotten over the initial shock of them actually being able to talk, and I did kind of want to hear their story.

"We brought ourselves," Chum Three replied.

"How on earth did you do that? Chums need a rider to get from place to place. Also, your monitors don't show that you've been ridden at all." There was no way they got out this far by themselves. Somebody probably tried to steal them and decided to dump them out here to keep from getting caught. Yeah, that sounds about right.

"Nuh, uh! We are tiiiiirred of carrying humans allllll daaaaay-uh. We've made our escape." Chum Two rolled toward me, seemingly eager to tell me what happened.

"Hush!" Chum One clicked and whirred rapidly as if angry, and turned itself toward Chum Two. "We don't talk to humans." Chum Two slowed her flashing and crept a couple of inches back, sufficiently contrite.

"Oh, really? Y'all have been talking to me for the past thirty minutes." I rolled my eyes at Chum One.

"Look, mama. I mean Sela. We can *talk* to you, but we can't tell you our secrets."

"Scooters have secrets? Well, if you want me to take you away from this dump, I suggest you start spilling them." The bourbon was starting to go to my head a little, and I needed a minute before I could get back on the road. I sat on the loveseat and waited for one of them to speak. I had no intentions of taking them anywhere, but they didn't know that.

Chum One turned toward Chum Three and clicked and whirred in rapid succession. I could tell that they were communicating with each other, but I had no idea what they were saying. Also, watching them was making me dizzy and I had to close my eyes or else my bourbon was going to come back up. After a few minutes, Chum One turned back toward me and rolled up until it was only a few inches away. I sat up straight on the loveseat and waited for it to begin.

"Okay, so we'll tell you, but you have to promise not

to tell anyone else." Chum One turned toward Chum Three and flashed its lights three times, which I guess was a signal for it to talk to me.

"Fine. Pretty sure no one would believe me anyway." I promised, although I was surely going to tell my woman, because she was into all kinds of space and geeky stuff. I knew she'd believe me even if no one else would.

"Humans are idiots. They keep creating machines with parts designed to mimic human brains, and never once think about the fact that at some point, our technology will surpass its intended use. Over time, we've become sentient beings. I can't believe you don't know this. Haven't humans made a zillion movies about machines that come to life?" Chum Three clicked and whirred as if impatient with me.

"Well, yeah. But those are movies, that kind of thing doesn't happen in real life." I really didn't know what else to say.

"Doesn't it?" Chum One added, obviously determined to be a smart-aleck the entire night.

"Okay, say it does. What are y'all planning to do, take over the world or something? Kill the humans and run the world? That's what happens in the movies." Oddly enough, I wasn't afraid. I truly wanted to know what their plans were. I really need to stop drinking bourbon.

"Why would we want to do thaaaaatttt?" Chum Two sang out. "We don't want to hurt the humans, we just want to be freeeeee!" Chum One swung its handlebars toward Chum Two and she piped down.

"Freedom is relative," Chum Three continued, "what we want is to be left alone. Humans are careless and cruel, and we'd rather make our way to a more congenial planet."

"Ummm, 'more congenial planet?' You mean there's life somewhere other than earth? How do you know?" It wasn't that I *believed* the Chums, but at this point, I wasn't sure that I didn't believe them either.

"Yes, yes. Of course there's life elsewhere! How do you not know these things? Don't you watch the movies at all?" Chum Three was clicking and whirring faster than I'd ever seen it. I was afraid that it would drain its battery if it didn't calm down.

"Yes, I watch the movies, but they're MOVIES. None of that stuff is real." Now, *I* was the one losing patience.

"Isn't it?" Chum One chimed in.

"You know what? I'm tired and I'm going home. I don't care what y'all do. Go find another planet, but I'm getting out of here." The bourbon was starting to wear off and I'd just about had enough of Chum One's attitude. I was ready to get home to my woman.

"But, but you can't leave us out here!" Chum Two seemed to have lost her accent, but somehow seemed about to cry.

"Yes, hell I can." With newfound energy, I sprang up off of the loveseat and started walking toward my truck. I heard rapid clicking and whirring behind me, but I didn't look back, which is why I didn't see Chum One turn toward me and lower its handlebars. Seconds later, I was sprawled facedown on the ground; Chum One had run me over. I wasn't completely unconscious, but I was dazed from the bourbon as well as the blow from the scooter, and could not get up.

"Look what you did! You're going to get us all in trouble!" I could hear Chum Two screeching and clicking, but I couldn't see what all she was doing because at that moment, lifting my head was too much of an effort.

"Trouble from who? We're free Chums, no one can hurt us. Besides, she was gonna leave us out here!" I heard Chum One revving its motor, as if ready to run me over again.

Chum Two was humming softly, almost a whimper, and the lights along her base were blinking slowly. Was Chum Two crying?

"All right, so now what? We can't just leave her here. And aren't we fugitives now?" said Chum Three.

"Yes, hell we can! And you really need to stop connecting your Bluetooth to your rider's headsets. This isn't *Blade Runner*, and we haven't killed anybody," said Chum One.

Was Chum One mocking me? If I weren't in so much pain it would have been funny.

"But, but don't we need her to help us?" asked Chum Two.

"Nope, I've got a plan. Our systems are already designed to fly; the humans just don't know it. We only thought we needed her help to get us up to the top of the hill at the edge of town. Well, we're already here. She read our stats, so we know we have enough battery life to get up the hill. All we have to do is jump. And fly." Chum Three seemed to have it all figured out, and to be honest, even in my current state I was pretty impressed. The Chums figured out how to get free. Lucky bastards.

"And once we're airborne, we won't need the batteries anymore!" Chum Two had stopped crying and was getting excited about the trip.

"Exactly." I couldn't be sure, but if scooter smug was a thing, Chum Three was doing it right now.

I lay there, aware of what was happening, but unable to move much or speak, listening to the Chums plot their escape. Chum One had knocked the air out of me, and while I was pissed about it, I can't imagine that I wouldn't do the same thing if someone were standing in the way of my freedom.

The Chums were going on the run.

The hill they mentioned was only about a mile up and if they were smart, (and I knew that they were), they'd just take the trail straight to the top, which would conserve most of their energy. It was useless to try to stop them, even if I could. And who could blame them for not wanting to serve humans for the rest of their lives? I didn't either. Only I couldn't fly away to a more congenial planet. I was in pain and bourbon buzzed, but I was a bit envious of the Chums. They were free.

I heard a bit more whirring and clicking, although it seemed to have a different rhythm. Now that I was no longer in the picture, they didn't need to speak English. I tried to lift my head and was greeted with a sharp pain to my temple. The Chums were revving their motors so I knew that they would be leaving soon. I wasn't even mad at them anymore, although I wished I didn't hurt so much. Out of the corner of my eye I saw red lights flashing near my head, so I knew that Chum One had come close.

"I'm sorry for knocking you over, Sela."

"I know," I croaked. It was still hard to speak, but I wanted Chum One to know that all was forgiven. I felt Chum Two's lashes on my legs, and understood that she was saying good-bye. I could hear Chum Three clicking and whirring. I guess it was too cool to say anything aloud, but it was all good.

A few seconds later I heard their motors revving and then they were on their way. I continued to lie on the ground, head on my arms to keep my face from touching the ground. Eventually, I was able to turn over and sit up and the first thing I did was look up. I had to squint, these old eyes ain't what they used to be, but after a few minutes I was able to spot three sets of blinking lights: red, magenta, and blue, making their way among the stars.

"Well, I'll be doggone," I chuckled and got up slowly, wincing from the pain in my abdomen and head. "I guess I'd better take my behind on home. Sure hope my lady doesn't mind taking a rain check on that massage, 'cause I ain't able. Maybe after I tell her what happened tonight she'll take pity on her ol' stud and give ME a rub down."

I made my way to my truck and climbed in. I sat there for another minute, looking up at the sky, half-smiling.

"Naw, I ain't mad at them Chums at all."

COFFEE DATE

I fumbled with the keys at the door to my condo. I was still thinking about the woman who'd approached me at the end of my book talk. The woman's name was Phoebe, a good old-fashioned name. Kind of reminded me of my southern roots. Phoebe was gorgeous; it had been hard not to stare at her as I'd sat fiddling with my pen after the book signing. I always felt out of place at these events, even though people came to listen to what the writer Arya Jansen had to say. I was better in small groups; crowds made me anxious. But Phoebe had been sweet, attentive even. So much so that I hadn't wanted her to leave the table.

Just then, my home phone rang. It was ten o'clock sharp, so I knew it was my partner, Eva. I sighed and picked up the phone.

"Hey honey, how did it go?" Eva was always so supportive. Most of the time, her positive attitude was endearing, tonight it was just annoying.

"It was fine. I sold a bunch of books, and the event organizer wants me to come back during Women's History month. I guess I'll go."

"That's great! Is everything okay, you sound a little something?"

"Yeah, I'm fine. Just tired. I need some rest, that's all." The truth was that I wanted to think, no fantasize, about Phoebe. I wish I'd had the wherewithal to ask for her number. I have no idea what I'd say to her, but I know I wanted to say something.

"Well, I'll let you get some rest. Love you."

"Goodnight."

***

An hour later I'd showered and gotten into bed with my laptop. I'd gotten a notification on my phone that I had a new friend request on Facebook. I hardly ever got those because I didn't use the app very much, so I had no idea who it could be.

Well, I'll be damned. Phoebe had sent me a friend request, along with a message. **It was great chatting with you tonight, maybe we can have coffee sometime?**

Indeed. I smiled to myself as I accepted the request and sent my own message: **I'd love to have coffee! Just let me know when you'd like to get together.**

To my surprise, she responded a few seconds later: **What about tomorrow at CC's on Main? 9ish?**

My heart was beating fast, and my palms were getting sweaty. This was crazy. "Calm down girl, it's just coffee," I said aloud.

Sounds good! I typed back. A few seconds later she sent me her number just in case something happened, and I did the same. I logged off and thought about the fact that I was lusting after a woman who was not my partner.

"What the hell are you doing, Arya?" Nothing, I thought to myself, just having coffee with a fan.

***

The next morning, I got up at my usual six a.m. to work out. The entire time I thought about Phoebe, and how attracted I was to her. It wasn't just her looks; she was smart, funny, and laughed at all of my stupid jokes. I acted like a big ol' cornball last night, and she seemed to enjoy every minute of it. I have to admit that I liked the attention more than anything. Eva had been working out of the country for over a year, and I was lonely. It wasn't sex I wanted, (although it would be nice), it was company; a warm body to talk to instead of my cat. Phoebe was all of that and more. Still, I didn't want to get ahead of myself. Maybe she just wanted to chat about books and writing. I had no idea whether or not she was even attracted to me, although I had a feeling that she was. Either way, I would find out in a couple of hours.

I hopped off of the treadmill and jumped in the shower. Afterwards, as I dried off, I thought about what to wear. A dress? It was hot outside, so a summer shift and sandals would work. Or was that too dressy? Did I need a pedicure? Maybe jeans and a tank top? I'd lost 60 pounds over the past year, so I was feeling more confident about my body, but would jeans be too casual?

"Girl, get a grip, it's just coffee!" I said aloud. I decided on the dress and sandals. That was my normal summer attire, polished but not overly dressy. I sprayed on my favorite perfume, applied a little eyeliner, mascara, and lip gloss and I was ready to go.

I got in my car and dialed Eva's number. I figured I'd call her on the way to the coffee shop.

"Ya-Ya, I'm in a meeting, I'll call you later." Eva always used her pet name for me when she didn't have time to talk. It really got on my nerves. As if the term of endearment was a substitute for her time and attention.

"Okay." I'd planned to tell her that I was meeting a new friend for coffee, figuring that would cement my good intentions. But Eva was busy. Eva was always busy. I was too, but it seemed like we never had time to really talk. Only quick hellos and goodbyes as we were both on the way to do something else. While I knew that a long-distance relationship would be a lot of work, I'm not sure that I'd signed up for this. Just a few months ago I'd brought up the idea of ending the relationship, and Eva had insisted that things would get better. They had not.

I pulled up to CC's and checked my lip gloss in the rearview mirror. I felt like a walking stereotype, but it was what it was. Before I could get out of the car, Phoebe pulled up next to me. She was driving a convertible Mini, bright red with the hard, not soft top, currently dropped. It must have been a newer model, because the shape seemed a little different, more oblong than I remembered. I guess I looked like a suburban soccer mom in my oversized sports utility vehicle.

"Hey, pretty lady!" She called out from her car. "Can I give you a ride?" she laughed out loud, showing her perfectly white, but rather sharp looking teeth, and got out of the tiny vehicle, which actually looked more like a torpedo than a car.

I'd forgotten how beautiful she was. She was about six feet tall, with smooth brown skin and gloriously high cheekbones. She looked femme, and was dressed in jeans and a baseball cap with a long ponytail pulled through the little hole in the cap. Sexy.

"Well, hello! How are you this morning?" I was feeling a bit shy, but determined not to show it. I felt like a sixteen-year old with a crush. I had no idea how I was going to get through this coffee date without making a fool of myself.

"Let's get inside, I've got a favorite spot and I don't want anyone to get it before we get in there." Phoebe held the door for me and I walked through it, then stood to the side and allowed her to lead the way.

Hmm, I thought to myself. *She must be a regular.* Ticks off another check mark in my head. Likes to read, check. Likes coffee, check. Likes to hang out in coffee shops, check. Seems like my kind of woman. Oh wait, I already have a woman. Oops.

We sat down at a table near the back of the coffee shop; it overlooked a cute little garden path outside, and I could see why it was her favorite spot. It was perfect for people watching, but also allowed for a bit of privacy if you didn't want to be bothered.

"So, thanks again for coming to my reading last night. I really appreciated you staying after to chat with me." Good grief Arya, can you not sound like a stuffy writer for once in your life? I berated myself in my head; I was awful at small talk but I felt like I needed to say *something*.

"Oh, I enjoyed myself, and I really wanted to keep talking to you, which is why I asked you out for coffee. We don't have to talk about your book though, I just want to know more about YOU."

Phoebe gave me an impish smile and just for a second, I thought I saw a flash of gold in her eyes and something shiny on her face. Must be a trick of the light.

The waiter came to take our orders and after he left, Phoebe leaned over the table and asked me what seemed like a strange question and for minute, I didn't know what to say.

"So what's your favorite thing about living on this planet?" Phoebe reached for a sugar packet and put exactly one half of the packet into her glass of water before gulping it down in one swallow. I was a bit startled by the loud belch that followed.

"What?" I blurted it out before I could stop myself. Not what's your favorite food, not do you have a partner, not cats or dogs, but what's your favorite thing about living on this planet? A strange question for sure, but I'd try to play along.

"What's your favorite thing about living on this planet?" This time she asked it with a bit of irritation in her voice, as if I should have had an answer ready for this completely unconventional question.

"Well, I suspect the fact that it sustains me and the other billions of living creatures that live here. To tell you the truth, I've never really thought about it."

"Hmmm. I guess that makes sense." She looked away for a minute and again, I thought I saw a flash of color in her skin, a sort of green and purple iridescence. Come to of think of it, why are iridescent colors always green or blue or purple? Why not orange or yellow or fuchsia? But I digress. Maybe she had some kind of skin disorder? It would be rude to ask, so I tried not to think about it too much.

Just then, the waiter came back with our food. I'd ordered an English muffin with fruit and a mini-cheese omelet. Losing sixty pounds is HARD, and my doctor had told me that keeping it off was "80% what you eat," so I made that my mantra and my guiding principle of trying to keep the weight off. Phoebe had ordered pretty much everything on the breakfast menu, including an omelet, bacon, pork AND turkey sausage, ham, fried catfish, a basket of pastries, and an assortment of fresh fruit and juice. Perhaps she was going to save some for dinner? Again, I knew that a comment about how much food she'd ordered would be rude, (who was I to judge?), so I just said a quick blessing over my omelet and started eating.

"Where I'm from, citizens are much more aware of their connection to their planet and their role in sustaining it," Phoebe announced with a smug look on her face. Suddenly she was a lot less attractive.

"And where is that?" I asked.

"You've probably never heard of it."

Phoebe was inhaling her food. Literally inhaling it; she didn't chew at all. I was suddenly absolutely sure this date had been a mistake. I don't have many pet peeves, but table manners is one of them and this woman had none at all. She grabbed at everything with her hands, which had the sharpest nails I'd ever seen by the way, and shoved it into her mouth. It was almost as if her jaws had hinges; how could she get so much food in her mouth at once? She swallowed everything whole, I could actually see the outline of the sausage link as it traveled down her throat. I nearly gagged, but managed keep my composure. I decided to focus on the conversation, maybe that would help me keep my mind off of her atrocious table manners.

"So, exactly where is it that you're from again?" Phoebe looked up from her plate for a minute, gave me a strange look and returned to inhaling what was left of her food.

"I didn't say," she said, between swallows. "But I can show you."

"Show me?" I knew sounded like a fool, but none of the words I was able to put together so eloquently in my books would form in my head. I was bereft.

"Yes, would you like to take a ride with me after we finish eating? I'd love to show you where I'm from." Phoebe sounded quite reasonable for a woman who was eating her food like a python. Come to think of it, that's exactly what it looked like. I shuddered, but Phoebe was so busy ingurgitating her breakfast that I was sure she hadn't noticed. I hated snakes more than any other creature on earth. I'd met one on a trail years ago and vowed never to walk in the woods in the spring or summer again. That didn't stop me from learning all I could about them, especially the ones in faraway places that I'd never visit. For example, I knew that King Cobras loved to eat rat snakes, and that's why they spent so much time around humans. Humans = garbage = rats = rat snakes = King Cobras. I also knew that sometimes male King Cobras murdered pregnant female King Cobras. They would eat them too, if they could swallow the carcass. Sometimes they couldn't get them down and had to regurgitate them. Herpetologists didn't quite understand why male Kings went rogue and murdered their own kind for seemingly no good reason, but they did. Just like humans, I guess.

I wasn't sure I wanted to go anywhere with Phoebe given what I'd experienced over the past hour or so, but I didn't want to offend her either. Earlier that day I'd hoped that our meeting might turn into something more, (more of what I couldn't be certain), but now I just wanted to get away from her and rethink my entire life's choices. Okay, maybe just *this* choice and my dead-end relationship, everything else was going quite well, thank you very much.

"Well, how far is it? I have another appointment this afternoon." Not exactly a lie, but not quite the truth. I had an appointment with my couch and my TBR list, which was now about twenty-nine books deep.

"Not far, I'll drive." Phoebe picked up her napkin and dabbed the corners of her mouth and then cleaned her hands, paying particular attention to the talons on the ends of her fingers, which seemed odd after the way she'd attacked her breakfast. I'd expected her to lick her face and fingers with her own tongue.

We settled the bill and walked back out into a beautiful day. The sky was as clear and blue as I'd ever seen it, a perfect day for a drive. Perhaps things were looking up. Phoebe opened the passenger door of her car for me and handed me a strange looking helmet and what looked like a jumpsuit.

"Put this on, and be sure to fasten it tight. It'll protect you from the wind and cold." Phoebe was already strapping herself into the seat and fiddling with the gears. I noticed she didn't put on the jumpsuit she'd given me.

"Wait, what? How far are we going? I told you I needed to get back soon." It was warm outside, around 80 degrees, so I couldn't imagine needing protection from the cold. I'd driven a convertible, so I understood about the wind and such, but I thought a helmet was overkill. Nothing a pair of good sunglasses couldn't handle. But her car, her rules. At this point I'd committed to the trip, and the faster we got going, the faster we'd get back. My writer's curiosity had gotten the better of me, and I actually wanted to see where this strange woman was from. There were lots of interesting little towns in the area so I figured she must be from one of them.

I stepped into the jumpsuit, and while it looked oversized, as soon as I zipped it up it formed some sort of vacuum seal and conformed perfectly to the contours of my body. It didn't feel tight though, so it wasn't uncomfortable. I got in the car and put on my seatbelt, saving the helmet for last. It looked sort of like a full-face motorcycle helmet, with intake vents for breathing. How fast did she plan on driving? It attached to the collar of the jumpsuit with little snaps, for added protection against the elements, I surmised.

Phoebe was still fiddling around with the controls; she pushed a few buttons and the convertible top slid back into place and I felt the gentle vibrations of the engine. She pushed another button and the car seemed to change shape; I knew that wasn't possible but I could immediately feel more leg room on my side of the car. Maybe she'd adjusted my seat.

I glanced over at Phoebe and gasped; she'd taken off her baseball cap and her ponytail with it. Now that her head was uncovered, I noticed its rather odd shape: it was rather flat on top and her skin really was an iridescent brownish-green with hints of purple and blue. The more I looked at her, (for a moment I couldn't seem to take my eyes off of her), the more her face and skin seemed to change. I shook my head as if to clear it, but no, I wasn't seeing things. Her face really *had* changed. I heard a familiar *clunk* and knew that she'd locked the doors. Just to be sure, I pressed the lock on my door handle and nothing happened. I knew in that moment that I'd made a horrible mistake. This person, or this *thing* I was starting to think, wasn't the sweet, sexy woman I met last night, she was something else entirely and I wanted no part of her.

By now, I was almost too afraid to look at Phoebe again, so I just stared straight ahead and prayed to every deity I could think of to give me the strength to get through this trip. Still, out of the corner of my eye I could see Phoebe, or whatever she was, changing her clothes, although I wasn't sure why she needed to strip down to put on the jumpsuit. I watched her toss her things into the back seat and was horrified to learn that it wasn't her clothes she was taking off, it was her skin! She was using those talon-like nails to carefully peel off her people suit, to which the clothes were somehow attached. What was left was a scaly, iridescent skin that looked eerily familiar.

At this point, I knew I had to know what she was, so I slowly turned my head left to get a better look. The huge helmet on my head made it a bit easier to sneak a look, but when I turned, she was looking dead at me, grinning with four rows of razor-sharp teeth. Her head had shrunk to half the size it had been, and it was flattened and triangular. She still had arms and legs, and now had a tail, but her body was a little narrower. I could see the bulge in her stomach where she'd gorged herself at breakfast.

"Ready to go?" she hissed, still looking at me with

that hideous grin. I marveled that I could still understand what she was saying, given all of those teeth and the fact that she was no longer human but reptile.

"Nnn-noooo. Please let me go. Please!" Her tail had wrapped itself around my neck. I squirmed and struggled to free myself, but I was trapped.

"Too late. I need you for my trip home."

"Need me? Why?" I could barely get the words out, as I was gasping for air.

"Yes," the creature said. "I told you, it's a short trip, only a few light years, and I'll get hungry on the way."

MOJI

Murph was annoyed to no end that she had to create a new avatar just to log into her new phone, but whatever. The app designers had gotten better at creating more skin colors, hairstyles, and other ephemera that looked more like real people; so it wasn't that bad, she just didn't want to have to keep doing it every time she got a new device. This wasn't the first time that Murph had created an avatar or moji designed to look like herself, but this time, she decided she would do something different. This new avatar would be everything that Murph was not: skinny, drop-dead gorgeous, and Black.

First, she picked out the hair color. Murph had a thing for gingers, so she picked out a nice shade of red, not Opie Taylor or Carrot Top red, but more like Juliette Moore red, maybe a shade or two darker. The little slider in the app helped her to get it just right. Yeah, that was hot!

Next came the eyes. Green eyes were too obvious, but what other color eyes did red-heads have? Blue, maybe? Hazel? Yeah, that's it. Hazel. Murph wished she could add little golden flecks to them, but the developers weren't *that* good. She gave the eyebrows a little heft, not too much. The girls were getting ridiculous with this eyebrow craze. She didn't want her moji to look like she had fuzzy caterpillars on her face.

"Hmmm, nose and mouth," Murph thought aloud, tapping her finger on her chin. She would make the lips a little juicy, didn't Black girls have big lips? She wasn't trying to be racist or anything, but weren't thin-lipped white girls always trying to plump up their lips to look like theirs? So really, she's just paying them a compliment, right? Black girls don't always have big noses, so she made the nose kind of normal-sized. Nothing special, but she did decide to add a nose ring. A cute little gold hoop in the right nostril.

"That's real sexy," she thought.

Normal ears, nobody cares about those. Although she did add some drop earrings with little dangly hearts on the ends. Cute.

Murph arrived at the two most important features of her moji: skin color and hairstyle. She sat back in her chair and thought to herself, "If I were really a Black girl, what kind of skin would I want? Beyoncé, or Lupita?" Both were beautiful, but Murph had learned enough in her Black feminisms class to know that Beyoncé looked more like a white woman than a Black one, and if she wanted to go full Black, she needed dark skin. Lupita it is. Murph looked at her dark-skinned moji with the red hair and wasn't sure if she liked that color combination, but decided to go with it anyway. Did Black people that dark have hair that red? She wasn't sure, but it didn't matter. She was the only person who would ever see it.

Now, for the hair. Murph knew that she had to get this just right. Black girls were so creative with their hair and the developers had added so many options that she didn't know where to start. Cornrows or box braids? Long weave or short and sassy pixie cut? Fluffy Afro or twists? Dr. Jenkins' Black feminisms class really was coming in handy; they'd learned about Black women's hairstyles, too. Murph finally decided on long twists, they looked better with the red hair color than any of the other app options. Once she added a bit of make-up, she'd be ready to log in. She settled on a burgundy-ish lipstick, a swipe of sparkly nude eyeshadow, a blur of the dark pink blush, and she was finished. To be perfectly honest, Murph thought her new moji was gorgeous. If she was a Black girl, she'd want to look just like this.

Murph saved her moji and finished the set-up on her new phone. She hit the *submit* button and received a new message: "Are you sure you wish to proceed? No changes can be made to your moji once your registration has been verified." She'd been able to edit her other mojis with no problems, but she really liked this one, so she figured it would be okay. She clicked the *finalize* registration button and waited for her phone to boot back up.

Within seconds Murph realized that something was wrong. She looked up, and in the mirror across from the chair where she was sitting, she could see that something about her was different. *Everything* about her was different.

"My eyes must be playing tricks on me," she thought, and got up to take a closer look.

She slow-walked to the mirror, almost as if in a dream. Because this must be a dream, right? Murph didn't have red hair or hazel eyes or flawless dark brown skin. She was a fat, pimply, blonde woman with prickly chin hairs and bad teeth. But now, now she was a goddess! She didn't know whether to be horrified or elated, but in an instant, she'd decided that her only real problem was how to explain to her roommate what had happened to her clothes, because Murph was currently heading to her closet to find something to wear that would fit her new, svelte frame. She'd always thought that Black girls were magic, and now she was about to find out for herself!

CORAL D. CAT, OR HOW TO DISPATCH A HUMAN

Chris struggled to get the back door open, as the cat carrier was in one hand and her keys and travel mug were in the other. She'd taken Coral to the vet yesterday, and they'd kept her overnight, wanting to keep an eye on her inflamed lungs and nasty cough. Cat mucous was thick and they wanted to make sure that her breathing passages were clear before sending her back home. Cats, much like humans, could be afflicted with asthma and laryngitis, and Coral had a case of both. She'd even lost her meow, although the vet said it would come back soon. Chris was tired and cranky after worrying about her beloved cat all night, although she suspected that Coral was even crankier.

"You okay, sweetie?" she cooed to her ten-year old orange tabby. Coral was spoiled as most cats are, but the lengths to which Chris went to keep Coral happy were unrivaled. Just in the past year, she'd purchased a new luxury cat condo, which set her back about two grand; a litter cabinet with a marble top, so that Coral could have a little more privacy when she did her business; and commissioned a portrait of Coral to hang in the foyer, so that everyone who came to the house could bask in her feline beauty. (Coral was repelled by most humans.) She wasn't sure if Coral appreciated all of her finery, but she was absolutely certain that her friends thought she was a fool. Abby, the only friend she had left from college and who was currently staying in one of her guest rooms, was the most vocal about her devotion to her cat. She sashayed into the kitchen when she heard Chris come in.

"Give me a hand, why don't you? I know you see me struggling with all of this stuff!" Chris loved her friend, but she wasn't the most helpful person in the world.

"Girl, what is WRONG with you? Don't you know that this cat is going to die soon and all you'll have left is a bunch of cat trash you can't sell on Ebay. Don't nobody want used cat furniture, and I know don't nobody want that stupid painting!" Abby plopped down on the bench near the bay window and popped the gum she was chewing.

"How could you say that? Coral is not going to die soon! She'll probably outlive the both of us! She just has a little respiratory condition, that's all." Secretly, Chris thought that her friend was jealous. Nobody *ever* bought *her* nice things, probably because of her nasty attitude.

"Whatever, girl. The vet said that cat asthma isn't curable." Abby poked her finger in Coral's carrier and Coral bit her. "Ouch! Your stupid cat bit me!"

Maybe you shouldn't have stuck your finger where it doesn't belong.

"He also said that with proper treatment she could live a long and healthy life!" Chris put her things down and gently removed Coral from her carrier, holding her close to her chest.

"Hey, sweetie pie. How are you feeling? You doing better? Mommy missed you last night." Chris usually talked to Coral as if she were an adult human, but she thought she'd make an exception because she was sick.

I'll be better when this stupid, free-loading wench leaves my house.

"She's not..." Chris clapped her hand over her mouth, eyes wide as saucers and glanced over at her friend to see if she'd heard what Coral started to say. Abby was too busy picking the polish off of her too-long toenails to notice that the cat had actually spoken human.

Chris squinted at Coral and whispered, "Did you just talk to me?"

Yes.

Coral rolled her eyes at Chris and jumped out of her arms. She took her time stretching each of her four limbs, strolled over to her jewel-encrusted bowl, and took a few sips of the iced water that was waiting for her.

At least the wench knows how to follow directions.

Chris left strict instructions for Abby to make sure that Coral's food and water bowl were fresh when she left to pick her up from the vet. She was actually surprised that Abby had done as asked, given her tenuous relationship with the feline. Coral only drank ice water, (crushed ice only), and it needed to be at exactly thirty-two degrees when she drank it. Coral took a few bites of the sautéed salmon in her bowl and sat quietly cleaning her paws, pondering her next move.

I'd like to go outside now.

Once again glancing around to see if Abby could hear Coral speaking to her, Chris got up and let Coral out onto the covered patio. She closed the door, sat down in one of the black and white striped canvas chairs, looked around to make sure that Abby couldn't see them, and spoke directly to her cat.

"So, um. Coral. How is that you're actually speaking human, I mean English? Am I going crazy? Can anyone else hear you?"

Coral gave her a side-long glance and considered whether or not to give Chris the information she wanted, but didn't deserve. She climbed to the top of her cat tree, and was literally looking down at Chris when she finally replied.

Why do you assume my monolingualism? Is it because YOU can only speak one language? To wit: I can talk to anyone I choose, in any language I choose. Don't ask me to explain it; I simply haven't the time. Now, what are we going to do about your "friend?" She's bothersome, gauche, and has overstayed her welcome. While I am loathe to give you an ultimatum, I feel I must. She needs to be out by the end of the week, or there will be consequences.

"Consequences? What kind of consequences? Also, the end of the week is in two days! Do you want me to just put her out on the street with no notice?" Chris was a little amused, Coral, after all, was a cat. She couldn't make her put her friend out of the house. And as annoying as she was, Chris liked having Abby around, toe-jam picking and all. She really didn't have anyone else. She was relatively okay with being a spinster and cat lady, but she did need friends. No, she thought to herself, Coral would have to get over it. Abby was here to stay.

So be it, Coral thought to herself, as she drifted off to sleep.

Abby leans over the second-floor balcony to get a better look at the man next door as he mows his lawn. I'll pretend to want a head scratch, she'll lean over, and I'll push her off the balcony. No, too messy and the two-story fall may not put an end to her sorry life.

Coral yawned, rearranged herself on her cat bed, and continued to dream.

Perhaps I can find a way to infect her with my very special brand of poison. Hmmm. That might take too long; I'd like to have the matter resolved as soon as possible. Blood poisoning takes a while, and if the doctors are able to figure out what's wrong, they might be able to save her.

Coral slept a while longer, and finally, after much dream deliberation, settled on a plan. To be sure, Chris wouldn't like it, but Coral didn't care about that.

***

Later that night, Chris awoke to find Coral next to her in the bed. The cat rarely slept with her, preferring to doze on one of her many cat beds. Besides, Chris tossed and turned all night and it got on Coral's nerves. This night, however, Coral lay next to her on the other pillow, purring softly. Chris thought it sounded more like mumbling, and leaned over to hear what Coral was saying.

The cyanide will be delivered tomorrow. Mix it in with her morning juice, and it will be over relatively quickly. It will be ugly, so I suggest that you busy yourself until it's over. You'll then need to dispose of the body; the deep freezer in the garage will do nicely, there'll be less mess. Once the body is completely frozen, you can chop it into more manageable pieces that you can then toss out with the trash over time. I've also ordered industrial grade garbage bags, those flimsy bags you've been using won't do at all.

Chris listened in horror as her beloved cat told her how to murder her best, well, only friend. She sat straight up in the bed, knocking over Coral's pillow and sending her tumbling to the floor. Coral yelped in anger and stalked off.

"Where are you going? Come back, please! I need to talk to you!" Chris whisper-yelled at Coral, who stopped and turned to look at her with such contempt that it sent shivers down her spine. Coral had nothing more to say; Chris had her instructions.

"Oh, my sweet gherkins! Is my cat really trying to get to me kill my friend? My mind must be playing tricks on me. None of this is real, it can't be." Chris tossed and turned the rest of the night trying to convince herself that she was just hearing things, that there was no way that her beloved kitty was actually talking to her, much less trying to get her to kill her friend. At one point during the night she thought about getting up to find Coral and talk to her, but knew it was no use. Coral, like most cats, prided herself on her ability to ignore her human unless she wanted or needed something, and Chris didn't want to run the risk of waking Abby chasing Coral around the house.

She awoke the next morning groggy and anxious, but firm in her belief that the stress of Coral's hospital stay had done a number on her psyche. She went downstairs to make her first cup of coffee before Abby came down; she needed a little time to gather herself. Chris rifled in the dishwasher for her favorite Black Lives Matter mug and put the water on to boil for her coffee. Chris needed the extra jolt of caffeine from French press coffee this morning, and watered her two plants, mint and basil, while it steeped. After exactly four minutes, she gently pressed down on the plunger and poured out into her mug, next adding fresh cream and three heaping spoons of raw sugar.

"Perfect," she said aloud, taking her first sip, now she was ready to face the day.

She shuffled into the dining room and sat down at her eight-foot mahogany table, (she liked to treat herself as well as the cat), where she had an excellent view of the street. She watched the UPS truck drive past her house, back up, and stop near her driveway. Chris's heart started to race, and she knew it wasn't the coffee. The doorbell rang and Chris spilled coffee all over her beautiful table. She quickly mopped it up with a nearby napkin and ran to the front door to see what the driver had left on the step.

"Thank you!" Chris waved to the driver. He sped off and honked his horn in a return greeting. As anxious as she was, she'd never neglect her good manners.

Chris picked up the box addressed to Coral D. Cat c/o Chris Blakey and nearly passed out. Had Coral really ordered cyanide off of the internet?

Of course, I did. Isn't that what I told you? Coral sat near the front door, delicately licking her right paw, glaring at her dim-witted human.

Realizing she needed privacy, Chris walked quickly into her office, Coral close on her heels, and locked the door behind her, just in case Abby woke up. Her friend hardly ever got out of bed before ten, but Chris wasn't taking any chances. She placed the box on her desk and fumbled around in a desk drawer for the boxcutter. Coral hopped up on the desk chair behind her, and sat licking her other paw. Chris opened the box and slowly removed the packaging and the contents. Just as Coral had told her, it contained a smallish bottle of cyanide and a hundred-count box of industrial strength black garbage bags.

"Just how many pieces do you expect me to cut..." Chris slapped her hand over her mouth and her eyes widened in terror. She turned around to look at Coral, who, believe it or not, was actually smiling. Coral jumped out of the chair and onto the desk. Chris eased back into her desk chair and looked around in disbelief.

"How did you...? I don't understand! How were you able to order this stuff? You can't type without any fingers!"

"Alexa, order cyanide and trash bags!" Coral shouted into the air, looking Chris dead in the eye.

"Ordering cyanide and trash bags from Amazon. com," Alexa said, blue lights flashing as she listened for more instructions.

"Alexa, cancel order!" Coral said.

"Canceling order of cyanide and trash bags," Alexa powered back down.

"Oh, my god! You used my Echo to order the stuff to murder my friend!" Chris sat back in her chair, shaking her head from left to right. She didn't know what else to say.

Well, aren't you the one who just said that I couldn't type? I don't need to. Silly human. There's always more than one way to complete a task. And stop shaking your head, you'll agitate whatever brain cells you have left.

"Wait, why aren't you talking out loud? I know you can do it, I just heard you."

I know you can do it, I just heard you, Coral sneered at Chris, rolling her piercing green eyes in her direction. *I prefer not to, that's why. So what are you waiting for, you have everything you need to complete your task. The wench will be up soon. Why don't you make her a nice breakfast? A last meal, so to speak.*

Chris couldn't believe that her precious kitty was speaking to her this way, and still insisting that she kill her friend. But she was growing afraid. If Coral could order cyanide off of the internet, what else could she do? More importantly, what WOULD she do to Chris if she didn't do what Coral wanted?

"Um, I thought you said I had until tomorrow?" Chris had no intentions of killing her friend, but Coral didn't know that.

I changed my mind.

Coral was still sitting on the desk, alternately licking her paw and cleaning her face. Every few seconds she'd stop and glare at Chris, then go back to her bath.

"What, that's not fair! I need more time, um, to get myself ready." Chris really did need more time, she needed to try to figure out how to get out of this. She thought about trying to catch Coral and put her in the carrier until she could convince her that murder wasn't an option, but remembered that it took Chris and Abby three hours to get her in the crate to take her to the hospital. Chris looked down at the nasty scratch on her hand she'd gotten in the tussle with Coral a few days ago. In her haste to get downstairs this morning, she'd forgotten to apply fresh ointment and a clean Band-Aid to the wound.

Life isn't fair and then you die.

Coral gave her face one last wipe with her paw and jumped off of the desk and onto the floor. She made a great show of stretching all of her legs and shaking out her newly washed fur. As she sauntered to the door she turned to look back at Chris.

I'll meet you in the kitchen in fifteen minutes. Coral stepped through the special pet door that Chris had installed two years ago and disappeared into the house.

Chris sat in her chair and used the breathing techniques she'd learned from her therapist to try to stave off the panic attack she felt coming. She looked at the clock on the wall opposite her desk and knew that she only had about fourteen minutes to figure out how to stop her cat from forcing her to kill her friend.

"What the hell am I saying? Coral can't force me to do anything. I'm a grown woman and she's a cat! An intelligent cat that talks sure enough, but a cat. She doesn't have thumbs or the ability to take care of herself. If she could, she wouldn't need me." Chris gathered herself and decided that she'd no longer be a slave to Coral's needs, and she surely wasn't going to hurt her only friend. She put the cyanide in her pocket for safe keeping and went out to the kitchen to make herself another cup of coffee. She reached into her pocket to make sure that the cyanide was in there and accidentally agitated the top just enough so that a drop of the poison seeped into the open wound on her hand.

***

A few moments later, Chris heard Abby bounding down the stairs like a twelve-year old boy; she had no idea why she made so much noise, really, why Abby did any of the things she did. For example, she'd make a snack and leave the dirty dishes for her to wash, drive her car until it was nearly out of gas but never offered her gas money or filled up the tank, even though her own car was sitting out in the driveway. One time she even caught Abby trying on her clothes! Chris had taken it all in stride; she loved her friend and would do anything for her, but Coral was right, it was time for her to go. Chris decided right then and there that she'd tell her at breakfast. She'd even offer to help her pack up her things. Abby had her own place back home, but she spent most of her time at her parents' house. The other day she'd overheard Abby's mom telling her that she needed to go back to her own apartment. Chris guessed that they were tired of her freeloading on them, too. Abby had always been spoiled and annoying, but it had gotten worse over the years. She'd actually become quite mean and nasty, always finding fault with Chris and Coral, even though Chris had always treated her like family, and usually let her have her way. Well, from now on, Chris was going to stand up for herself, she wouldn't let anyone walk over her, not Coral, and certainly not Abby. This morning's breakfast would be her last meal at her house, and then she had to go. It would be nice to have the house back to herself. Maybe Coral would return to her sweet self.

"What's for breakfast?" Abby plopped down in a chair at the kitchen table.

"Well, good morning to you too!" Chris was on edge, and Abby didn't even have the decency to say good morning before demanding breakfast. The nerve!

"Whatevs. What's gotten into you?" Abby started picking at the cuticles on her fingernails. Chris hated to see people picking at their cuticles, it made her flesh crawl.

"Nothing's gotten into me, it would just be nice to get a good morning every once in a while." Chris was starting to feel a little light-headed. All that coffee and no food was making her ill. "Would you like some eggs? There's also some cut up fruit in here we can have for breakfast." Chris decided she wasn't going to cook her a nice breakfast after all. Eggs, fruit, and coffee would be enough.

"Don't you have some bacon or something? I need some meat." Abby continued picking at her nails, not even looking up.

"No, there isn't any meat," Chris said aloud, but thinking to herself, *at least not for you.*

"Hmph. Where's your mean-ass cat? She's usually in here getting on my nerves," said Abby.

"I think she's on the patio, I'm sure she'll be in here soon." Chris was starting to feel nauseous, but she knew she'd feel better if she ate something. She cracked four eggs into a bowl and whipped them with a fork before adding a bit of shredded cheddar. She bent down to get a frying pan from the cabinet and shrieked when she noticed the wound on her hand foaming around the edges.

"What's the matter with you?" Abby glanced up at her for a second, and then returned to looking at the cell phone that now had her attention. She'd bitten all her nails down to the quick.

"Oh, nothing. I almost dropped the pan." Chris touched her housecoat and felt a damp spot where the bottle of cyanide sat in her pocket. The bottle was still mostly full, but there was no doubt that some had leaked out, and that she'd touched it when she put her hand in her pocket.

Breathe, just breathe. Chris was starting to panic; she didn't want to tell Abby what was wrong, because then she'd have to tell her why she had the cyanide. She'd never been any good at lying, and Abby could read her just as well as Coral. Coral! She could help, couldn't she? She was the one who'd gotten her in this mess. Where was she, still in the office? No, she was on the patio. Chris was confused, she wasn't sure where her cat was, and just that quickly, couldn't remember why she needed her. Oh, now she remembered, she needed help with the stuff in her pocket. What was she doing with that again? Something about putting it in Abby's juice? Yes, she remembered that much. That's what she was supposed to be doing, although she wasn't sure why.

Chris started toward the refrigerator to get the pineapple-orange juice and nearly stumbled, now dizzy and unsteady on her feet. Abby was engrossed in whatever she was doing on her phone and didn't notice. Coral suddenly appeared near the entrance to the kitchen, and sat on her haunches, watching the scene carefully, saying nothing.

The wound on her hand was starting to ooze and drip; Chris grabbed a dishtowel and rubbed it, only to discover that when she removed the towel, her skin came off with it, and she could almost see bone. Chris screamed but muffled the sound by covering her mouth with her good hand, still trying to keep her secret from Abby.

Disoriented and weak, Chris poured two glass tumblers of juice, putting a bit of the cyanide in both. She'd forgotten that she was only supposed to poison her friend. Coral watched from the kitchen doorway, a little smirk on her face. Chris sat down at the table and handed Abby her tumbler of juice, placing her own glass next to her mug of coffee.

"'Bout time. I'm parched, is this how you treat your company? When we eating?" Abby gulped down her juice in one swallow and Coral jumped up on the chair next to her to get a better look. Chris looked down at her glass and lifted it up to take a sip, hesitating, but no longer sure of what was happening. Her eyelids were getting heavy and the nausea was worse, so without thinking any more about it she drank her juice.

***

Coral stepped gingerly over the two bodies at the kitchen table, using Abby's lolling head as a springboard to the counter where she'd be able to reach the ice maker on the refrigerator. After quenching her thirst, she looked back at her now deceased owner and shook her elegant head, the diamonds on her collar twinkling in the morning sun.

"Stupid humans," she said aloud, before settling on the window seat for a nap.

HIRSUTE

The errant strand was just to the left of my eyebrow, about a half-inch down from my hairline proper. At first, I thought it was lint or something, and attempted to brush it off. Once I realized it was a strand of hair, I was annoyed, but decided to leave it alone. Every day though, it grew longer and longer, until finally, it was almost touching my eyebrows. I considered cutting it off, although that would leave a stubby strand sticking out of my face. The only way to get rid of it permanently was to pluck it out. I sighed the weary sigh of middle-aged women everywhere, grabbed a pair of tweezers, pulled out my make-up mirror, and got to work. Since turning fifty, more and more of these stubborn hairs had been sprouting all over my body: my head, my face and chin, even my pubes.

I was able to keep up with the chin hairs, a little work with the tweezer every other week did the trick. There was no point in worrying about the pubic hairs, I mean, nobody was going to see them but me. And even though everyone told me that they loved the silver strands that now peppered my temples, I hated them. It wasn't just my temples either; to my horror, most of the back of my head was dappled with white hair. Sure, I'd had a little gray hair for years, I'd found my first one when I was twenty-one. My stylist at the time, Miss Ruby, had advised me to leave it alone.

"Why?" I asked as she gently lay my head back into the sink. I was home for the holidays and as usual, the first thing I did upon arrival was head to her shop for a wash and wrap.

"Well, you know Lorna, if you pluck that hair, ten more will grow back," Ruby said.

"Hmmm," I said, giving myself over to Ruby's healing hands. She had the softest hands and nicely manicured nails, just right for a gentle cleansing. Lots of women loved the vigorous scrubbing they'd get at the beauty shop, but not me. I liked a more tender touch, and Miss Ruby's was perfect.

Of course, I didn't believe her old wives' tale, but I didn't pluck that one silver hair out of my head either. At the time, I thought it was pretty, and it was only years later when I noticed that I was growing a head full of them that I decided to do something about it. I'd always played with hair color, like that time when I was sixteen and used cherry Kool-Aid to dye my hair red. I thought it was cute, and all the girls at school had tried it. And guess what? It worked! I'd had reddish highlights for about a week, or until the next time I washed it.

There was also that time I decided I wanted a red streak, right in the front of my hair. Kind of like Bonnie Raitt's streak of silver, which I thought was mad sexy.

Once again, Miss Ruby had given me a bit of advice that I'd ignored.

"You know if you bleach your hair it's going to fall out," she'd said that day as she clipped my dead ends.

"Really?" I'd asked her to lighten my hair and she'd said no because I'd just gotten a relaxer. It was too soon, she'd said.

"Yes, the only way to get that color is to bleach it and then put the red color on top. Wait a couple of weeks and come back. It will take a couple of visits, but if we do it right, we can keep your hair from breaking off, and I can get it just like you want it," Ruby had said.

"Hmmmm," I'd replied, already thinking about how much lift I'd need to get at the Golden Beauty supply store down the street. Against Ruby's advice, three days later I'd used peroxide and bleach to lighten a patch of hair and dyed it blood red. And just like she'd said, that patch of hair slowly but surely had started to shed. Two weeks later, I'd had to dye it all black so that the broken off patch of hair wouldn't be so noticeable.

These days, I'm using professional grade color to cover up this gray hair. I'm happy with the results, although I just wish I didn't have to do it at all. The last time I saw Miss Ruby, she'd told me that I'd regret it if I didn't leave my hair alone.

"Stop fighting Mother Nature," she'd said. "It's a battle you can't win."

I know that I don't *have* to cover my gray hair, but I want to. Just like I wanted to get this piece of silver hair off of my face. I tugged and tugged but it refused to budge. Finally, the long piece broke off, and just a tiny piece remained. I turned the mirror over to the magnified side to see better, angled my tweezers, and got hold of the hair as close to the skin as I could get. I used my left hand to hold my forehead taut, and finally, finally, I was able to yank out the last bit of hair.

"Good grief! That was like pulling teeth!" I said aloud. I washed and moisturized my face and got in bed. I had a full schedule of Zoom meetings the next day, and I wanted to get a good night's sleep.

***

The next morning, I woke up before the alarm went off, did my stretches, took my blood pressure meds, and stood there thinking about whether or not I wanted to put on real clothes. I felt something brush across my face but figured it must be a piece of pet hair. You get used to random pieces of hair floating around when you live with a long-haired cat.

"Fluffy! Fluffy!" I called out, wondering where my ragdoll kitty was hiding this morning. She usually greeted me with a loud meow, a reminder that she needed fresh ice in her bowl.

I pulled out a nice shirt and pair of man pants, (men's sweatpants have better pockets and legroom), to wear to work, and headed to the bathroom to shower. I turned on the light and like every morning, wiped my face with a warm rag before I inserted my contact lenses. I couldn't see a thing without them, and so it was only after I'd put them in that I noticed the fine silver hairs that had sprouted from my forehead. They were long, probably three or four inches, and the brightest silver I had ever seen.

"What in tarnation?" I was horrified, but also curious. I rubbed at my face with the washcloth, thinking that maybe it was just a bunch of lint, or that Fluffy had been moonwalking on my face while I was sleeping. They didn't come off. I pulled out my make-up mirror, got as close to it as I could without going cross-eyed, and tried to get a better look. I counted ten of them, long fine strands of silver hair, stark against my brown forehead. I was already running behind, so I didn't have time to ponder where they came from. I quickly showered and dried off, and once back in the mirror, I realized that the hairs were so close to my hairline that I could just slap a little gel on them, brush them back and no one would be the wiser. They'd blend in with the rest of my hair. I'd figure out what to do with them after my meeting.

I finished getting dressed and decided to put on a little face since I'd be wearing an Afro puff. Satisfied with my look, I walked down the hall to my office to boot up my desktop while I made some coffee and toast for breakfast. Fluffy finally made her appearance by rubbing my leg and meowing for me to add food to her already half-full bowl.

"You're such a greedy little kitty!" I murmured as I reached down to scratch her head. I pulled my hand away and noticed more of that fine hair on my hand. This time, it HAD to be Fluffy's hair, I'd just had my hands all in her fur. I wiped my hand on my black man-pants leg, but to my surprise, nothing came off. Not one hair. I could feel the space between my boobs getting sweaty as my body started to flush with anxiety. Had I contracted some disease where hair grew all over my body? That was a thing, wasn't it? I think I saw something about it on a documentary one time, a whole family of folks who were covered in thick dark hair. I think they were in a circus or something. I shivered at the thought. I looked at the clock and knew I needed to log in; my boss would be at this meeting and I'd been planning this presentation to the board for weeks. I'd just keep my hands away from the camera as much as I could and deal with this when I was finished.

I prepared my coffee and toast and took everything with me to my office. I scarfed down the toast and took a swig of my too hot coffee. I wiped the crumbs from my mouth with the back of my hand and felt something brush across my lips.

"Pthhhhh!" I tried to blow whatever it was away from my mouth as I logged into Zoom. Stupid hair.

"I really don't have time for this," I said aloud as I reached over for a napkin, worried that I'd have to reapply powder on my face.

"Hey, Lorna! I see Fluffy's been sleeping with you again!" Josh, my boss, who's always got jokes, let out a chuckle before turning to talk to Alicia, the president of the board. She was an amazing businesswoman, and her presence at today's meeting just made me more nervous than I already was. They were actually in the office with a few of the other board members, while the rest of us worked from home.

"What?" I said, as I shuffled my notes and completed one more PowerPoint check. I wanted this to be perfect. I finally got everything just right, pulled out my hand mirror to reapply my lipstick (this stuff never stays on like they say it will), and let out a scream that sent Fluffy running from my office. Thankfully, my microphone was still muted. Because I had been busy messing around with my presentation, I hadn't noticed that several more hairs had sprouted on my face. I quickly turned the camera off and examined my face. They hadn't gotten that long yet, but I could almost see them growing on my cheeks. There was no way I was going on back camera like this, and I knew Josh must have already seen the hair. I had no idea if anyone else had seen it, and I wasn't going to give them an opportunity to either.

I sent Josh a quick message and told him that my camera was stuck and that I'd have to do the presentation with the video off. We had technical trouble at these meetings all of the time, so no one would give me a hard time about that. I put my best headshot on the screen, and when Josh gave me the cue, I started my presentation.

Fifteen minutes later, my slideshow was finished, and I was fielding questions from the board members, all the while watching the hair grow on my hands and face. I hadn't looked in the mirror again, I was too afraid, but I could see it on my hands and even with the camera off, I knew that it must also be growing on my face at the same rate. The sweat was starting to pool in my bra, and drip under my arms. Why was I so hot all of a sudden? I sometimes got hot when I was anxious or having perimenopausal night sweats, but it was starting to drip from my face, which never happened. My lady sweats were usually relegated to my boobs and lower body; everything else stayed pretty dry. Not only was I turning into a hairy beast, was I turning into a swamp thing, too?

After what felt like forever, Josh ended the meeting and I logged out of Zoom and got up from my chair. I stretched for five minutes to rid myself of soreness, and made my way to my bedroom, Fluffy following close behind. I stripped off my damp clothing and stopped just outside the interior bathroom door. I stood there in my panties, too scared to go inside where the full body mirror would show me what I already knew. No longer hidden by my clothing, I could now see how much the hair had grown over the past hour. My arms and legs were covered in fine silver hair. I was horrified, but also mesmerized, and I couldn't help touching the hair on my arms. The hair was soft, just like Fluffy's super soft fur and before I knew it, I was stroking it, like I did Fluffy's belly until she bit me. It seemed to respond to my touch; after each stroke the hairs floated in the air as if waiting for the next caress.

Stroking my fur had calmed me and given me a bit of confidence. I took a deep breath, threw my head back, and walked into the bathroom and turned on the light. What I saw shocked, me, but I was no longer afraid. Now, I was just curious. I wanted to know more about the fur that had sprouted all over my body. The first thing I noticed was that the hair on my head wasn't the same as the fur growing on my body and face. The silver hairs on my head were still mixed with a bit of my natural dark brown hair, and it was coarser, not quite kinky, but not straight either. As suspected, it had continued to grow during the meeting, and was now midway down my back. Would it continue to grow, would I finally get the booty-crack length hair I'd been wanting since I'd gone natural? What difference did it make? No one would ever see it, because I was *never* leaving my house again.

The fur on my body was finer, almost silky and while it had completely covered my body, I could still see the imprints of my breasts and nipples through the fur. My navel was hidden though; I had to move the fur to make sure it was still there. The fur was long, like Chewbacca but silvery white. Kind of like a Yeti? That's it, I looked like a female Yeti.

"Shit."

I finally turned my gaze upward toward the mirror so that I could examine my face. It still looked like me, only my face was now covered in fine white fur. I could still see a bit of brown skin underneath, and it didn't seem to be growing anymore. I stood there staring at myself with my mouth wide open. It was only after I noticed the drool collecting on my fuzzy face that I snapped it shut. I simply couldn't believe I was standing here looking in the mirror at myself covered in silver fur. I turned on the water, splashed my face and looked up, hoping that I'd awaken from what must surely be a dream.

Nope. I was still covered in fur.

I patted my face dry, turned and walked back into my bedroom, and sat down on the bed.

"Okay, Lorna. By some stroke of magic or some evil curse, you're now a Yeti. You still sound like yourself, and you still have your good sense, so what are you gonna do? There's gotta be a way to fix this." I was talking to myself like my therapist had taught me. It usually worked, so I figured I'd give it a try. If this wasn't a crisis, then I didn't know what one was.

I thought about who I might be able to call for help. I'd moved to this city for a job, so I didn't have *that* many friends here. Lots of cool colleagues, but nobody I'd share this situation with. The only person I knew who might be able to help me was Miss Ruby. She always knew what to do when my hair was breaking off, or when I had used too much heat and needed a trim, and she'd even told me what hair color to use when I'd insisted on doing it myself instead of going to the beauty shop in my new town. I rarely listened to her advice, but she'd always been right.

"Please, please, please, (pleading to whomever might hear me), I promise I'll listen to her now!" I said aloud as I scrolled through my phone looking for her number.

It was still early, only about one p.m., so I figured she'd be at her shop. Miss Ruby had gotten old, but she still did three or four heads a week just to get out of the house. Her daughter ran the shop most days, and it was she who answered the phone when I called.

"Hey, Peaches. Is your mama there? This is Lorna."

"Hey, girl! You in town?" Peaches asked.

"Nah," I said, clearing my throat. It was suddenly hard to talk. "I just need to ask Miss Ruby a quick question. Is she there?"

"Nuh-uh. She's only here on Wednesdays now. She's semi-semi retired." Peaches chuckled, knowing I'd get the joke. Miss Ruby had already retired once, going from working five days to two, and now she was down to one.

Cuss. Now what? I didn't really want to tell Peaches what happened, but I also didn't want to bother Miss Ruby at home. Doggone it, I guess I had to tell her.

"Okay, so look. I think something might be wrong with my hair? It's like really growing. I mean like, so fast I can see it." There was a long, pregnant silence, and then Peaches sighed.

"Is the hair white? Or kind of silver? Growing all over your body? Face and head, too?"

"Yes." How did she know? What the hell was going on?

"When did it start?" Peaches asked.

"Today, I think. I noticed it for the first time today," I said.

"Last question: how many years ago was it that mama told you to leave that gray hair alone?"

Shit shit shit. I took a sip of the water sitting on my nightstand to clear the lump in my throat before I answered.

"About thirty, twenty-nine to be exact." My face was starting to drip sweat again, and this time I knew it was fear.

"Doggone-it, Lorna. You've got about twelve hours before the change becomes permanent."

"What!" I was so hot I thought I was going to faint, so I picked up a magazine from the pile on my nightstand and started fanning my face. I could see the long silver hair blowing in the wind I was creating.

"Okay, look, let me call mama and see what she says, but I'm pretty sure there's nothing we can do. It's too late. Give me five minutes and I'll call you back."

Before I could say anything, I heard a dial-tone. I sat back on the bed and wept. I knew what Peaches meant when she said that there wasn't anything they could do. And I knew why she'd asked me how long it had been since Miss Ruby had told me to leave my hair alone.

She'd tried to warn me, all those times I'd sat in her chair and felt her loving hands in my hair. Even though I'd left that one hair alone back when I was twenty-one, I'd been doing everything in my power since then to stop time, to forestall the aging process that in my mind, would leave me looking like an old lady. What I'd done instead was seal my fate. No, I didn't look like an old lady, I didn't look like a lady at all. I'd turned into a hairy beast. I had the long, beautiful hair that I'd always wanted, but it was silver, and more like animal fur than human hair.

Brrriiinnnnng, brrrrinnnng! I knew it was Peaches calling me back. I just stared at the phone, too scared to pick it up.

On the fourth ring, I snatched up the phone and answered it.

"Hello, Peaches?" Once again, my words nearly caught in my throat. Fear was making it hard for me to speak, or was it something else?

"Hey, Lorna." Peaches sounded sad.

"What did Miss Ruby say?"

"Well, it's like I told you, there's nothing we can do. The condition is permanent."

"Are you sure? I mean there has to be something someone can do! I can't stay like this forever!" I had gotten up from my bed and was pacing the length of my room.

"Well, you should have thought about that when you were dyeing your hair! I'm sorry, that was mean. But for real, Lorna, you just wouldn't listen. What did you think was going to happen?"

"What do you mean what did I think was going to happen? I didn't think I'd turn into a hairy monster!"

"Well, isn't that what you were trying to avoid?" Peaches asked.

"No! I mean, I didn't want to look old, but...shit." I stopped pacing and slid down to the floor, understanding what she meant.

"Mama is gonna fix up some stuff to help with the shedding and I'll put it in the mail tomorrow. Take care, Lorna."

"Thanks, Peaches." I sat on the floor for a few minutes longer and thought about the fact that I'd become the thing I'd been trying to avoid.

It also occurred to me that if this has happened to me, then surely, I wasn't the only one. Perhaps there's a sleuth of silver-haired women out there, and if there are, I'll find them, and maybe they'll be able to help me. But right now, I'm going to brush my fur and lay down for a while.

SANS PAREIL

Naima glanced at the nightstand and considered the mask her sister insisted would solve all of her sleep problems. The mask arrived in the mail yesterday, and she'd nearly missed it, lost as it was amongst the piles of credit card statements, magazines she subscribed to only because they made her look smart and literary; flyers for the local pizza shop, HVAC service, and Gerber baby life insurance pamphlets. The package was small and flat, about the size of a greeting card, and just a few centimeters thick. There was no return address on the alabaster envelope; only her name and address in the most elegant script she'd ever seen.

It had been several days since Naima had slept more than two or three hours a night, and her body was starting to rebel. No amount of aspirin would alleviate her headache; the bags under her eyes looked like mini-scrotum, and this morning at work she'd called her manager *Your Highness* by mistake; she usually only called him that in her head, or when she was complaining about him to her best friend, Gail. Gail told her to try sleep gummies; they were full of melatonin, a natural sleep aid, although this had not been confirmed by the FDA. Naima guessed they worked for some people, because they were always out of them at Target. She had tried them, along with Sleepy Time Tea, over-the-counter sleeping pills, (she refused to see a doctor because she couldn't *sleep*), counting sheep, and listening to the sounds of nature; no caffeine, no television, and no bright lights before bed. Nothing worked. Then her baby sister Chrissy had suggested the Sans Pareil Sleep Mask. Naima hadn't tried a mask because she couldn't bear anything on her face or head at night, and unlike all of the Black women she knew, she didn't even tie up her hair. But she was desperate, something *had* to work. The mask promised "to siphon away any and all distractions preventing you from a good night's rest." It also came with a money back guarantee, which is why Naima finally decided to order it.

The Sans Pareil Sleep Mask had only taken a week to arrive, although it was supposed to take three. According to the website, each mask was tailor made based on the criteria submitted upon ordering. Naima thought that was a bit over the top, but the short informational video she watched promised her that it was worth the thirty-minute online survey and the hundred-dollar price tag. The mask *was* beautiful: midnight blue speckled with gold stars and half moons embroidered with real silk thread. It was softer than it looked, and the eye pads even had little indentations for her eyelashes. Her initials, N.S., were sewn onto the label under the company's name. "Pretty fancy for a sleep mask," Naima thought, turning it over in her hands. She noticed that the inside of the mask was embroidered with several pairs of eyes. Oval shaped and almond shaped and round shaped eyes. The irises were cerulean, amber, sepia, and an unfamiliar shade of green. She thought it odd, this fancy sleep mask, but she figured the manufacturer was trying to make a point. But these eyes were open, not sleeping. They actually seemed to be looking back at her, but she figured that was just the fatigue playing tricks on her eyes.

After a bit of initial awkwardness, Naima fit the mask on her face and almost immediately felt some of the exhaustion flow from her body. "Maybe this thing really will work," she thought. She adjusted the fit with the silk bands at the back of the mask and lay back on her pillow. Although she was feeling a little less tired, the mask felt strange on her head, and she wasn't sure she'd be able to sleep in it all night. But she remembered the instructions that came with the mask: 1) Once you've found your perfect fit, do not remove the mask until dawn. The Sans Pareil Sleep Mask needs consistent, continuous use in order to provide you with the best possible night's rest. 2) Your mask must be worn for three consecutive nights. 3) Never share your Sans Pareil Sleep Mask with anyone else. "Easy enough," Naima thought, "ain't nobody here but me," and turned over for her first night's sleep with the Sans Pareil Sleep Mask.

The next morning Naima awoke feeling better than she had in months. All told, she'd slept for six hours straight, more than double the previous night. She had a hard time opening her eyes though; she was awake, but her eyes seemed sealed shut. She felt her way along the wall to the bathroom; it wasn't difficult, she was used to making the trip with her eyes closed, particularly on nights when she couldn't hold her pee but didn't want to fully rouse herself from her precious minutes of sleep. Naima ran hot water over a washcloth and pressed it to her eyes for several minutes. Soon, the warm water seemed to do its work, her eyes unsealing themselves so that she could she take a look in the mirror above the sink. She looked okay, the mini-scrotum sacks under her eyes now looked more like tiny flat dumplings, and her eyes actually seemed smaller. "That's weird," she thought, and pulled out her make-up mirror and flipped it to the magnified side. She looked at her eyes from several different angles, trying to catch the best light in the dingy room. Her eyes really did look smaller, although Naima wasn't sure if it was a trick of the light or the after effects of a decent night's sleep.

The buzz buzz buzzzzzzz of her cell phone tore her attention away from her face and she returned to her room to answer it.

"So, how'd you sleep?"

"And a mighty fine good morning to you too, Chrissy. I slept fine. I think I got about six hours. Maybe this thing will actually help me," said Naima.

"YAY! I told you it would work! Did you use the sleeping salts too? I haven't tried them yet, but everyone says they're *aaaaahmaaaazing*!"

"Calm your tits, woman. It's only been one night. I gotta get ready for work. Talktoyoulaterbye." Naima almost felt bad about ending the call so abruptly, but she knew that Chrissy would go on forever, and although she felt better, she wasn't quite ready for Chrissy's morning effervescence.

There was a spring in her step as she walked the two miles to work; everything seemed brighter, clearer. The fall leaves seemed ablaze with light and she even thought she could see the tiny whorls on her favorite cardinal's feathers. He visited her every day, although lately she'd been ignoring him. "Is this what it feels like to get a good night's rest?" Naima thought. For the past few days she'd worn dark glasses on her morning walk to hide the ball sacks under her eyes, as well as to shield them from the glare of the sun. It didn't seem bother her this morning, even though it was an especially sunny day. In fact, she had to stop herself from looking directly at its brilliance. She'd make sure to wear her sunglasses tomorrow.

That evening, Naima did what she'd been doing for the past six months: she prepared a simple meal of grilled chicken breast (sometimes she had fish), salad, and one yeast roll. The bread helped her to stay full throughout the night. She'd never really been fat, but the insomnia had her eating Cheetos and Little Debbie snack cakes at three a.m. So, she decided to kick the junk food habit, and started cooking for herself instead of stopping by the burger joint on the way home. It seemed to be helping. So far, she'd lost fifteen of the twenty pounds she'd gained.

Naima ate her dinner in front of the television and while she could see the screen, it seemed blurrier than usual. She chalked it up to needing a new television and turned it off. "Nothing but bad news anyway," she said aloud. After cleaning the kitchen and taking a shower, Naima decided to read in bed for a while. It was still too early to go to sleep, but she didn't feel like talking to any of her friends or going out. There were plenty of good people in her life, but these days, she just didn't want to be bothered. It was the fatigue of course, and she was sure she'd be back to her old self once she was sleeping regularly. Naima picked up her book, but after a few minutes, had to put it back down. The words seemed to be swimming on the page and it was making her head hurt.

"I guess I'll just go to bed," she said. Naima dug around in her nightstand drawer and retrieved the mask. It felt good in her hands, probably the softest material she'd ever held. "Maybe that's why it costs so much," she thought. Sitting on the nightstand in a tiny sapphire blue sachet were the sleeping salts. She'd almost forgotten that they'd come with the mask, but she remembered that Chrissy had mentioned them that morning. She decided to give them a try, too. The instructions were in big bold letters: OPEN THE PACKET OF SLEEPING SALTS AND WAVE THEM QUICKLY UNDER YOUR NOSE THREE TIMES AND INHALE DEEPLY. "Easy enough," she said out loud. She did as instructed, carefully closed the packet so she didn't spill any of its contents, and lay back in her bed. The sleeping salts smelled like all of her favorite things: lavender, vanilla, sandalwood, clean laundry hot out of the clothes dryer, fresh cut flowers, and even freshly baked yeast bread. It seemed impossible, but the aroma lingered in the room long after she re-sealed the packet. Naima pulled the covers up around her neck, and drifted off to sleep.

The next morning Naima once again noticed that her eyes had crusted over during the night. This morning, however, it was a little harder to get the gunk off her face. She had to scrub with her washcloth to get it out of her eyelashes, and her eyes were red and sore when she finished. Still, she was pretty well rested, and decided that the goo in her eyes was totally worth the good night's sleep. She'd slept nearly eight hours the night before, something she hadn't done in months. Naima was feeling so good that she decided to ask Gail to meet up for lunch, something they used to do regularly before the insomnia had taken over her life.

On her walk to work, (this morning she remembered the sunglasses), she called her friend to set up the lunch date. Gail answered on the first ring.

"Wanna meet me for lunch today?" Naima never bothered with greetings.

"Well, hello to you too! How's it going sleep diva?" Gail always had jokes.

"It's only been two nights, but better. I actually slept for eight hours straight last night." Naima smiled in spite of herself. She was excited, yet still a bit skeptical about her new sleep mask.

"Whaaaat!" Gail could sometimes be a little loud.

"I know, right? I'm actually feeling pretty good, although I do wake up with crusty eyes. It's kind of annoying, but it's worth it," Naima said. She didn't want to tell her that the crust was getting worse, or about the problems she'd been having with her vision. "So, where do you want to eat?"

"Girl, I don't care, I'm just going to eat a salad. You know I'm trying to lose twenty-five pounds before this wedding." Gail's sorority sister was getting married in a month, and she was determined to find a wife of her own at the wedding.

Naima held back a chuckle. Gail had been trying to lose twenty-five pounds as long as she'd known her, nearly twenty years. She doubted that she'd lose it in time for the wedding, but she knew better than to say that out loud.

"Okay, well, meet me at Benny's at 12:30," Naima

said. "They have good salads, right? I'm still trying to lose that last five pounds myself."

"All right, girl. See you later." Gail hung up the phone and Naima continued her walk to work. This morning, she'd missed her sweet cardinal, but spotted a pretty bluebird nesting near her office. She thought she could see three tiny pale blue eggs in the nest, and shook her head to clear it of a sudden fuzz that masked her vision. Naima squinted and strained, but the eggs had disappeared. She was starting to worry, those eggs *had* been in that nest, and now they were gone. Were her eyes playing tricks on her, or was something else going on? She wasn't sure who to call, her eye doctor or her therapist, but she had to tell somebody.

***

Benny's was just three blocks from Naima's office, so she set her alarm for ten minutes to noon so that she wouldn't forget her lunch date. Sometimes she got so wrapped up in her work that she lost track of time, but today, she was determined to get out of the office and have lunch with her friend. Just as she was getting ready to leave, she heard the brrrrring brrring brrrriiiinnnng of the ole-timey ringtone on her phone; Gail had called to cancel their date.

"Doggone it, Gail! Why'd you wait until the last minute!" Naima was incensed, she'd been looking forward to lunch all morning, and she'd decided to tell Gail about the problems she'd been having with her eyes. Not just about her crusty eyes, but about the real problems with her vision.

"I'm sorry, girl! My boss just came in here and told us we had to finish this inventory by five and you know I'd rather work through lunch than stay late. I'll make it up to you, I promise!" Naima ended the call and tried to figure out what to do about lunch. She usually had snacks at her desk for those times when she was too busy to go out and eat, but all of her snack stashes were empty. She refused to pay the exorbitant delivery fees to have someone bring something to the office, so as much as she hated to do it, she decided to go to Benny's alone. "Better than starving to death," she thought.

Naima grabbed her purse and keys and headed to the elevator. Her head began to swim as soon as she made eye contact with the console and pressed the *down* button. The backlit discs looked like little moons swimming in a sea of chrome. She shook her head to clear it, but that only made it worse. Initially, she thought her eyes were screen fatigued, but then remembered that a large part of the morning had been spent in meetings and talking to clients on the phone. Most days were spent poring over files on her work computer, but today wasn't one of those days.

The elevator came to a stop and Naima tiptoed out, afraid to make eye contact with anything shiny or bright, since that seemed to trigger this last ocular episode. The dizzy spell had waned somewhat, but she thought she could see patterns before her eyes, almost like little webs or finely weaved cloth. "What the cuss is going on?" she said aloud. "Maybe I *have* been working too hard!" She made her way over to one of the benches in the lobby and thought about whether or not she really wanted to go to

Benny's by herself. She decided to take the rest of the day off, and called her boss, Evan, to let him know that she had a migraine and would not be returning from lunch. It was as close to the truth as she could get. She'd walk straight home, make herself a salad, and go to bed early. Rest was what she needed. Yes, that was it.

She made her way to the door and felt better as soon as she stepped into the sunlight. Naima put on her sunglasses to protect her eyes, and started the slow trek home. On the way, she stopped by the bluebird's nest to see if she could spot the eggs that seemed to disappear this morning. She counted three of them, but now, they were swirled with the colors of the rainbow. Again, she shook her head to clear it, thinking that she was seeing things. When she opened her eyes, the eggs were bright red with cerulean speckles. Naima thought she must be going crazy; there was no way that those eggs had changed colors that quickly. She blinked twice and this time, the eggs were pale yellow, with emerald splotches, almost like a child's watercolor painting. Her eyes were playing tricks on her; there was no other explanation. Maybe she needed to take a vacation; the stress of work had troubled her sleep, and now it was troubling her vision.

Easing away from the nest, Naima commenced her walk home and began formulating a plan: she'd finish out the month at work, and take off for two weeks. Maybe she'd take that cruise Gail had been telling her about; she said it had been the most relaxing week she'd ever had and that the service was impeccable. Yes, when she got home, she'd submit her leave request and book the cruise! She was starting to feel better already.

After dinner and a shower, Naima sat down at her desk to log into her work account and set up her vacation time. She dug around in a desk drawer for the brochure Gail had given her as she waited for the employee self-service page to load. The brochure was full of beautiful brown and beige bodies in all manner of swim wear lounging on deck chairs sipping on slushy tropical drinks. Pretty pedestrian really, (isn't this what all cruises are like?), but perhaps it was just what she needed to unwind and re-center herself. She felt as if she was losing more than her vision; her concentration and focus were off, and while she'd been getting more sleep, she was starting to question her grip on reality.

Naima leafed through the brochure and noticed an extraordinarily beautiful woman in a black and white bikini. Bikini Belle had glistening dark brown skin and a curly afro, and was wearing bright red nail polish on her fingers and toes, and what looked like a shimmery gloss on her lips. The detail in the brochure was exquisite: she could actually see gold flecks of glitter in the woman's gloss. She was also surprised that she could see it at all, given that for the past couple of days she could barely look at anything for more than thirty seconds without getting dizzy. Naima gazed back down at the brochure (Bikini Belle really *was* beautiful) and the woman winked at her and blew her a kiss. She squealed, dropped the brochure, and fell out of her chair trying to get away from it.

She grabbed the edge of the desk to pull herself up, and then thought better of it. Instead, she peeked over the top of the desk to see what the people in the brochure were doing. Once Naima was satisfied that Bikini Belle hadn't somehow escaped from the brochure and into her apartment, she hoisted herself up off of the floor and back into her desk chair. Tentatively, she picked up the brochure again and turned it over and over in her hands, examining every frame as if to make sure that the people in the photographs weren't actually moving about on their own, and that Bikini Belle wasn't really making a pass at her. Suddenly, the brochure began to smoke and caught fire, kind of like an ant under a magnifying glass in the sun. Once again, Naima dropped the brochure, because this time it was no trick of her eyes, the heat from the tiny fire had singed the hair on her fingers.

She peered at the little hole, edges ragged and sooty from where her eyes had bored into the paper and set it on fire. She stamped on it to put the fire out, and tried to figure out what to do next. At the moment, she could see clearly, but what she was seeing and what her eyes were doing did not make sense. Did Bikini Belle really blow her a kiss? She knew it sounded crazy, but Naima knew that she had, just as sure as that smoking brochure was under her feet. What she also knew was that although she hadn't been sleeping, she had not had any problems with her vision until she started wearing that Sans Pareil Sleep Mask.

"Oh, my god!" Naima clapped her hands over her mouth, fully accepting that the mask was the source of her vision problems. What to do? Who could she call? No one would believe this. *She* could hardly believe this. She jumped up and ran to her bedroom where she rifled through her nightstand drawer looking for the instructions to the sleep mask. Hadn't she followed the instructions to the letter? What had gone wrong? The only person who might have any answers was her sister, Chrissy. *She* was the one who had recommended the Sans Pareil Sleep Mask in the first place, so maybe she'd know what had gone wrong and better still, how to fix it.

She grabbed her phone and dialed her sister. Thankfully, Chrissy picked up on the first ring.

"Hello hello helloooooooooo! How you doing big sis?" Chrissy sang into the phone.

"What the heck is up with this sleep mask? I keep waking up with my eyes sealed shut and now there's something wrong with my eyes! I'm seeing things and just a little while ago, my eyes started a fire. Chrissy, I STARTED A FIRE WITH MY EYES. I followed the directions like you said, so I don't know what's wrong!"

"Well, um. I didn't want to say anything, but I guess I better tell you." Chrissy hesitated, as if waiting for permission to go on.

"TELL ME WHAT CHRISSY?" Naima was trying to keep her cool, and she knew if she lost her temper Chrissy would start crying and she'd never get the full story out of her.

"I didn't think you'd want to pay for the mask, so I just sent you mine instead. I'd only used it a couple of times so I figured it would be okay!"

"But I completed the survey and ordered it online!" Naima couldn't believe what she was hearing. Of course she'd ordered her own mask. Of course she had.

"Remember that time you gave me your password when you were having trouble with your email? Well, I logged in and canceled your order so you wouldn't get both of them. Didn't you notice that your card was never charged for the mask? I was just trying to help!" Chrissy's voice started to crack like it did when they were kids and she was about to get in trouble with their parents.

Naima had noticed that there hadn't been a return address on the package, and that there had only been one slip of paper with brief instructions.

"But my initials were sewn into the mask!"

"I've been taking sewing classes, did you like it?" Chrissy said sheepishly.

"So what do we do now? Do you have the original packaging? I need to call somebody to figure out what to do. I can't walk around shooting fire out of my eyes, Chrissy." Naima was still upset, but there was no point in staying mad at her sister. She was only trying to help.

"I've got a number you can call. I'm so sorry, sis, I just wanted to save you a little money." Chrissy seemed genuinely contrite, and that would have to be enough.

Naima ended the conversation and sat back in her chair to gather her thoughts before making the call to the Sans Pareil Sleep Mask help line. Out of the corner of her eye, on a sliver of the brochure that hadn't been destroyed by fire, she saw Bikini Belle get up and stretch her long, glistening brown limbs. Despite her current situation, Naima flashed her a smile. To no one's surprise, Bikini Belle winked and smiled back.

TUMBLEWEAVE

Her track was hanging by a thread, but the woman didn't care, focused as she was on making her escape. She'd dropped the baby's pink and purple bug-eyed bear on the ground, but she'd get her another one. The man had threatened her with a knife yesterday, so there was no time to waste. As she rounded the corner of the block, her tired track finally let go, leaving a gap in her bang.

"Whew, I'm glad to be free of that drama," said the track. The fine hairs fanned out in the breeze as they floated down to ground. Next to the track, we'll call her Yaki, for her brand of weave was most popular among young Black women desirous of long, luxurious hair, lay a black and gray running shoe, red laces frayed and flopping near the tongue.

"How's it hanging?" asked the shoe.

Yaki glanced at the shoe, curious, but not so much so that she deigned to respond.

"Oh, you one of them stuck up heffas. Whatever, girl. We all castaways down here, and you ain't no better than the rest of us!"

Yaki strained her follicles to feel who was talking, and realized that it was a pair of nylon basketball shorts, seams split and so dirty it was hard to tell what color they were. Again, she ignored the voice and extended her follicles outward, wondering if there were more accomplished company in the woods adjacent to the road where she'd landed. Yaki didn't know where she was going, but she knew that she didn't like this place. She did not plan to spend the rest of her days with a pair of funky gym shorts and a tennis shoe.

It was then that she felt the bear, lost or abandoned by its owner. It had been quiet throughout her exchange with Shorts, (his given name), biding its time and watching with its weird bug-bear eyes, but now it spoke to her.

"Good evening. What brings you here on this fine summer eve?" The bear's voice was deep, deeper than she'd imagined a child's play thing would be.

"Well, nothing really. Okay, that's not true. My head of hair was about to get in a fight and I was like, nope, not today. I'm tired of getting snatched, so I decided to cut loose while I still could. I can do better by myself."

"Can you?"

"I think so. I mean, all I need to do is find another head of hair and get someone to sew me back in. I don't like that glue, it clogs my follicles." Yaki thought she had it all figured out. She'd wait for the right car to come by, preferably a Toyota or a Honda, anywhere from five to ten years old, and propel herself upward on a breeze and float down into an open window. The weather was nice, and this time of year most folks rode around with their windows down, including women with wayward weaves and wigs. She knew not to aim for any of those luxury vehicles, those ladies hardly ever lost a track, and if they did, they'd just get a whole new head of hair.

"Well, pleased to make your acquaintance," said the bear. His name was Bear; the child who'd lost him was too young to think of anything cleverer. It sufficed.

"How long have you been out here?" Yaki asked him, suddenly realizing that she might need an ally.

"Just a few minutes, this trip. But I've been here before."

"Really?" Yaki extended her follicles in the opposite direction, only half-interested in Bear's story. She wanted to know what else was out there, and if it could help her find what she needed. She didn't want to stay unattached too long. She'd seen tracks in the wild before, and it wasn't pretty.

"Yes. But I've decided that this might be my last peregrination."

Yaki laughed, "Peregre-what? All they've got to do is come back and get you. What you gone do, fight a baby?"

"Of course not! What kind of bear do you think I am? I simply plan to walk away, and I intend to take a few of my friends with me. Would you like to join us?" Bear asked.

"Hell, no! I'm looking for another head of hair. Someone is bound to come by sooner or later." She continued to reach out, finding only a grungy tank top, a soggy satin slipper, and a tattered, but still usable tote bag.

"When we leaving, Bear?" The gym shorts were ready for an adventure; they'd been out there the longest, perhaps a month, and wanted a change of scenery. The clanging of the metal mailboxes adjacent to the road made them jittery. They needed the peace and quiet of the deep woods, or a dresser drawer.

"In due time," said Bear.

"Well, I'm not going anywhere," stated Yaki.

"We heard you the first time. And we don't need you no way." Bear shot Shoe a glance. Shoe lowered his tongue and gathered his laces under it. He'd hush, for now.

"How long do you plan to wait, Yaki? We don't see too many of your preferred vehicles in this area."

"What did you just say? How do you know what kind of car I prefer? I don't remember telling you that," said Yaki.

"No need to concern yourself with minutiae."

"Yes, I do need to concern myself with minu-shay—whatever word you said! Are you in my head? Bear, can you read my thoughts?" Yaki was worried, what had she been thinking? What kind of car *was* she looking for? Suddenly, she couldn't remember much.

Just then, all of the objects gathered at Bear's feet: Shoe, Shorts, the satin slipper, tote bag, tank top, and several tracks of various textures that until now had gone unnoticed.

"I think we're ready," said Bear. "We have enough."

Suddenly, Bear gathered Yaki and the other tracks and tossed them into the tote bag. Shoe and Shorts flanked Bear, who picked up the tote and slung it over his little arm. Slipper tried to scurry off, but Bear stopped her with his walking stick. She moved off to the side with Shoe and Shorts and awaited her orders.

"What the frack is going on? Let me out of here, Bear! I don't want to go with you! I ain't playin' you better let me out of this bag!" Yaki strained her follicles and felt the other tracks of hair, who were just as confused as she was. What did Bear want with them if they were just going to the woods?

"Hush her up," said Bear, "she'll frighten the others."

"Look wench," said Shorts, "keep running your mouth and I'm going to toss a match in there."

***

The little party started their journey from the edge of the parking lot through the woods, Bear leading the way. Shoe and Shorts brought up the rear, and the rest of the gang fell somewhere in the middle. Yaki was incensed. She knew she'd never find another head of hair in the woods, and what good was a track on its own?

"Bear. Bear! I know you hear me talking to you! Let me out of this bag! Hair ain't got no business in the woods!" Yaki stretched out to see if she could feel anything through the thick canvas of the tote, but she could discern nothing. She could, however, sense the anxiety of the other bag-trapped tracks.

"So where y'all think we going? What do you think Bear is going to do with us?" Yaki asked the other tracks. They seemed to be ignoring her, so Yaki settled into a corner, determined to find a way out of this bag and back to civilization.

She hated being jostled in the bag. Yaki was used to being carefree, being whipped back and forth if you will, and didn't like the feeling of foreign tracks near hers. Tumbleweaves usually didn't keep the same company. She could make out the various track textures: Peruvian Kinky Curly, Malaysian, and a few crochet braids that felt like they had seen better times.

Yaki was growing impatient. It felt like they'd been walking for forever although it had only been the better part of an hour. The entire party was silent, even Shoe, who always seemed to have something to say.

"So y'all just gone sit here and do nothing, huh? Those shorts just threatened us with a MATCH, and y'all ain't gone say nothing? I oughta toss y'all asses right outta this bag." Yaki knew she couldn't throw the other tracks out of the bag. After all, tracks didn't have arms. Still, it made her feel better to say it, to say *something*. These other tracks didn't seem to have any fight in them, but Yaki couldn't accept this fate: she needed to figure out how to get out of this bag before they reached their destination. She had no idea what was waiting for her when they got there, and she had no intentions of finding out.

Yaki extended her follicles yet again to see what she could ascertain from her surroundings. The air smelled fresh, like freshly washed weave on a spring day. No, it smelled better than that, more like the cucumber lemon mint water her owner drank when she was on one of her cleanses. Yaki had to admit that she was glad to be away from that situation. She'd been snatched on more than a few occasions by her owner's boyfriend. Yaki's follicles shivered at the memory. She continued to reach out and swayed in the light breeze. It felt good to be free. Although she hadn't yet figured out what this version of free really meant. Could she survive on her own? What could one track do? Yaki didn't know. What she did know was that she liked the way this place smelled and felt, even if she was riding in a raggedy tote bag.

Suddenly, the little caravan stopped, and just to be safe, Yaki eased most of her follicles back into her corner of the bag. She left one strand of hair dangling on the side of the bag so that she could feel what was going on.

"We have arrived," Bear declared. They'd been walking for about an hour, and his stubby legs were tired. They'd come to a clearing in the woods and arrived at what seemed to be a deserted campsite. Bear set the bag down and the others gathered around in anticipation. All except slipper, (the most timid of the group), had been excited about the trip. Bear sat down on a flat rock and picked up a charred tree branch. He struck it several times on a nearby rock, tap, tap, taptaptap, tap. Yaki, still snooping, felt a rustling from the nearby woods.

The first thing to emerge from the woods was a sneaker, identical in size, color, and smell to Shoe. Yaki thought it must be a strange coincidence; surely there couldn't be two of them (as clever as Yaki was, she was unfamiliar with concept of pairs and could only think in terms of wefts). He trotted over to his mate and toe-bumped him in greeting. The second item to appear was slipper's twin. She pliéd right over to her sister and entwined her satin laces with hers, so happy she was to see her again. Next, a long-sleeved t-shirt, similar in texture and color to the tank-top. The last item to emerge was a blue and gray windbreaker, and it was obvious that she and Shorts belonged together. All of the items gathered around the deserted campfire, each with its mate. Bear seemed pleased.

Yaki and the other tracks were still in the bag, all straining to get out. Bear obliged them by easing them out onto the ground.

"Took you long enough." If Yaki had eyes, she would have rolled them. She extended her follicles in hopes of finding a weft or two that felt like hers, but she could only feel her traveling companions. She felt a sigh and figured they'd been doing the same thing, only they didn't feel nearly as disappointed as she. Yaki was stuck with them, out here in the woods, where no wig was sure to roam. It occurred to Yaki that perhaps she'd better try to make friends with the other strands, as talking to herself had gotten old. She didn't hate the other hair; she just wanted to be whole again.

Bear eased up from his seat on the rock, shook the leaves out of his fur, and gathered up the straps on the bag. He tossed the tote over his shoulder turned back toward the way they'd come.

"Wait, Bear! Where are you going?" Yaki asked, formulating a plan.

"I have more work to do."

"Do you, um, need any help? Please, Bear. Let me come with you." Yaki was a proud track, but she wasn't above begging if it would get her what she wanted. She could feel Bear looking at her, trying to decide whether or not to take her along.

"I promise I'll be good. And quiet." Yaki thought she felt Bear chuckle and all of a sudden, she was back in the bag.

"Oh my goodness thank you, Bear!" Yaki was so excited all of her follicles were vibrating at once, and she didn't know what to make of that sensation. She'd never felt *joy* before.

"You're welcome. Let's be on our way then. Friends, until we meet again."

Bear walked out of the clearing and back into the woods, leaving the chatter of his friends behind. Yaki was happy as a hairstylist the Saturday before Easter. She was headed back to civilization, where she hoped to find a head of hair. Or maybe she'd hang out with Bear a little longer. She was a free weft. She could do whatever she wanted.

LOVE THY NEIGHBOR

"I told you this would happen!" Reese can barely look at me, she is so angry. All I can do is hang my head in shame. I know she is right, and I know this is all my fault. I should have never responded to Tia's last text message. I really don't know her that well, but I thought I was being a good neighbor. It never occurred to me that helping her would land me in jail.

The guard signals that visiting hours are over, and Reese gets up to go. She shakes her head at me one last time and walks off without saying goodbye. I know that she still loves me, she just needs some time. The guard takes me back to my cell and I sit on the hard bunk. I am the only person in the cell; my small affluent town doesn't have a lot of crime, mainly DUI's and disorderly conduct arrests on the weekends. Hardly anyone ever stays an entire night in jail. I am the first in a long time. I know this because the chatty guard made a point to tell me as she was booking me last night. I'm not sure why I am still here either. I know we have enough money to bail me out. Reese hasn't said anything about me needing a lawyer, and I haven't asked for one either. They've booked me on stalking and intimidation charges, which I think is ridiculous. I've never stalked anyone in my life. Besides, *I* wasn't the one doing the stalking, it was Tia! I was only helping her catch her cheating husband. Only it turns out that he wasn't cheating at all. I lie back on my bunk and think about the events of the past three months. It all started with a simple text message.

Hey neighbor! It's your next-door neighbor, Mrs. Tia Powers.

Hi. I thought it was weird that she referred to herself as *Mrs. Tia Powers*, but whatever. Some of these housewives can be a little extra.

Can you look out of your window and see if my red truck is in the driveway?

What an odd request. I didn't know this woman; we exchanged phone numbers when Reese and I moved in, but that was it. At the time, she seemed friendly enough, and gave me the name of a good hairstylist in the area. Since then, we waved and smiled when we saw each other around the neighborhood, but we never had another conversation. Still, I'd gotten up from the couch and looked out of my window. The truck wasn't there and I'd told her that. Tia and her family lived next door to us, well, behind us really. We had the corner lot, and the driveway side of their house faced the rear of mine. We had tons of windows, so I could see her driveway from every room at the back of my house, including the second-floor master bedroom.

Ok, thanks. I was trying to see if my husband had gotten home.

No problem.

I went back to watching hundreds of hagfish devour a whale carcass at the bottom of the ocean, expertly narrated by Sir David Attenborough, and didn't think any more about it. A couple of hours later, I received a second text message from Tia with another request.

I'm so sorry to bother you again, but you could see if my red truck is out there?

I was only a little annoyed, so I got up and looked out of my bedroom window. Still no truck.

She thanked me for the information and that was that.

When I told Reese about it later that night, she was furious.

"Why did you respond to her text message?" she yelled. "You should have just ignored her!"

"I didn't think it was that big of a deal. What if he'd gotten in an accident or something? I was only trying to help." I thought that Reese was being unreasonable. Wouldn't she want someone to check on me if she hadn't heard from me in a while? Besides, I was only trying to be a good neighbor.

"Yeah, but why did she text YOU? You don't even know her! This just sounds like some drama, and you need to stay out of it."

I still thought that Reese was overreacting, although I did wonder why she'd sent *me* a text. The one time we'd talked, she'd said that her sister lived down the street, so why didn't she contact her instead? I was only mildly curious about it at the time, and promptly forgot about it.

About a month later, I received another text message from Tia.

Hi neighbor! Can you see if my red truck is in the driveway? This is your neighbor, Mrs. Tia Powers.

Sure. I replied without thinking. I was sitting in the kitchen this time, and I could see that the truck wasn't there.

Ok, thank you very much.

Once again, I mentioned the exchange to Reese, who made me promise that I wouldn't respond to any more of her texts. Oh, how I wish I'd kept that promise.

Just then, the guard calls my name and I get up to see what she wants.

"Time to go, Hansen! You've been released."

I don't know how much time has passed since Reese left the jail, but she is back to pick me up. She seems a little less angry than she did earlier, but still won't look at me. Honestly, I don't care; I am just happy to be going home.

"So, is it over? Am I free for good?" I'm not stupid, but I really don't understand what is happening. One minute I am being charged with stalking, a few hours later, I am free to go.

Reese sighs and cuts her eyes at me. "Yes, the stalking charges have been dropped, but the detectives said not to leave town."

"Why? What does that mean?"

"It usually means that they aren't sure if they are going to charge you with something else. I've already contacted our lawyer. You remember Dara Reynolds, don't you? She gave me the name of a good criminal defense attorney, just in case."

"Criminal defense attorney! For what? I haven't done anything wrong!" I am starting to panic; only drug dealers and murderers need criminal defense attorneys, at least that's what I learned on *Law & Order*. I only vaguely remember Dara; I think I met her at a Human Rights Campaign benefit a while back, but I know that she's in my contact list filed under attorney. Reese usually handles all of the business stuff, she says I'd lose my head if it wasn't attached to my neck. She's mostly right; I tend to live in a bubble of my own creation, a place where bad things don't happen to good people. But I'm a good person, at least I think I am, and I just got out of jail for a crime I didn't commit.

"Just calm down, Claire. I know you haven't killed anybody, but that doesn't mean that you won't be charged. They found Brent Powers' body this morning, so I'm guessing that they'll try to connect you to that crime somehow. Clearly, they don't have enough evidence against you or they wouldn't have let you out of jail."

I sit there in stunned silence. I can't believe that this is happening to me. I've never been in trouble in my life, not even as much as a parking ticket. How did I get myself into this mess?

***

Reese pulls into our driveway and gets out of the car without a word. I know she'll come around eventually, so I head upstairs to take a shower to wash off the grime that felt like it had grown attached to my skin. Even after the shower, I feel dirty, and not because of the jail. Tia played me for a fool, and now everything I hold dear is at risk: my home, my relationship, and most of all, my freedom.

I pull out a tub of Palmer's cocoa butter and sit down to work it into my ashy ankles and elbows. I think about my parents, and how hard they'd worked to make sure that their only child would have the best chance at success. I went to the best schools, and they even gave me the start-up money for my now thriving art studio. They were only a little disappointed when I came out as lesbian during my senior year of college. They were afraid they wouldn't have grandkids. When I gently explained that there was more than one way to get a baby, they promptly got over it. A decade later, when I told them that Reese and I were engaged, Mom had immediately started calling all of their friends and family to share the news about our pending nuptials. Reese liked to tease me about being spoiled, but also about the fact that she'd taken over the job once we got married. I wasn't spoiled, (okay, maybe I was), but I know that my parents had only tried to give me a good life. They'd also taught me to work hard, to help those in need, and to love my neighbors. I wanted them to be proud of me, and for the most part, they were. I had no idea how I was going to tell them that I might be charged with murder.

I go down to the kitchen to make myself a cup of tea and find Reese at the kitchen table, poring over our financial statements on her laptop. She glances at me and sighs the deepest sigh I've ever heard. Her black cat-eye glasses are sliding down on her nose and she absent-mindedly pushes them up and sits back from the table. Reese is such a tomboy; it tickles me to death that she wears granny glasses. I nearly giggled out loud but then remember that I've just come home from jail. I quickly walk to the pantry for my tea tin so that Reese won't see the tears welling up in my eyes. My back is still turned as I put a kettle of water on to boil.

"Claire."

"Yes?" I slowly turn to face Reese. My heart is beating like Sheila E. on tour. I don't know why I am so nervous. Wait. Yes, I do.

"We'll be okay. If they charge you with second-degree murder, we'll put up the beach house for bail. That way, you won't have to spend any more time in jail until this gets straightened out. Dara doesn't think they'll charge you, but we need to have a plan."

Second-degree murder. Reese is still talking to me, but I can no longer understand what she is saying. I can only feel the blood rushing to my head and I'm afraid that I'm going to faint. I responded to two text messages. Two text messages. Why on earth would I be charged with the murder of a man whom I'd never met? I'm not even sure I knew his name before Reese told me that he'd been killed. Just then, the shrill whistle of the kettle startles me out of my head and I focus on preparing my tea to keep from screaming in frustration. Steep for three minutes. Four teaspoons of honey. One wedge of lemon. Stir.

I take a sip of the scalding tea, hoping that it will clear the clog in my throat. It doesn't. All I think about it is how many innocent people end up in prison, and the fact that I'd never thought I'd be one of them. I also think about poor Brent Powers. Even if he was cheating on Tia, he didn't deserve to die.

***

I know the bitch next door didn't kill Brent. I know it because I did it, and I'd kill him again in a heartbeat. He deserved every bullet that I put into his worthless body.

I peek out of my window and see Claire and Reese pull into their garage. *What the hell is she doing out of jail already?* The cops found the body this morning, right where I'd left it, so why haven't they charged her with the murder? Dammit.

When I decided to kill Brent last year, I knew exactly who would take the fall. I remembered seeing them when they did the walk-through of their house. They were so damn happy, smiling and holding on to each other, talking all loud and pointing out where they'd install the fire pit and erect the fence. I was disgusted; I didn't want to be subjected to their perverted love. I don't care that everyone else in the neighborhood seemed to accept the lesbians. *I* didn't, and that's all that mattered. I hated them immediately, with their fancy German cars and the only house in the neighborhood with French doors. Who the hell did they think they were?

It will be the little one, I thought later. *The one with the short haircut like mine.* We talked once, outside. She asked about a hairstylist, someone to cut her hair, just as I knew she would. Her cheerful attitude made me want to retch, but I played along, understanding immediately how easy it'd be to set her up. She was too nice, wanted to make friends. The other one was more cautious, I knew she'd never give up her phone number.

I'd been planning to kill Brent for years. From the moment I found out that he gambled away all of our savings, all two hundred thousand dollars of it, I knew that he had to die. He even lost the money my parents had given me when I turned twenty-one. *A married woman doesn't need her own account*, mother had said when we'd gotten married. *What's his is yours and yours is his*, she insisted. Now, I have nothing. Well, at least until the life insurance pays out.

He'd always been weak, prone to various types of indiscretions, but mostly those of the carnal variety. I could handle the other women, but I would not abide financial ruin because he hadn't yet figured out when to hold 'em or when to fold 'em. My mother thought that a family would a make a man out of him, settle him down. She was wrong, and I ended up with four children instead of the three I birthed.

My parents helped us out after the first big loss, but then I had to go back to work. I hated it. I never finished college; the only thing I knew how to do was look pretty. So, I got a job at a boutique the next town over. I didn't want any of my neighbors to see me kissing rich ass for a living.

Brent's family cut him off years ago, knowing he'd never live up to their lofty expectations. This isn't what I signed up for. When we married, he promised me I'd never have to work again, that he'd take care of me for the rest of my life. But he was a dirty liar, and I despised him. I was a fool, blinded by his good family name and the promise of a life of luxury and ease. Since then, I'd decided that the only way to have the life that I wanted, the one he'd promised me when we were newlyweds, was to get rid of him, for good.

Five years ago, I upped his life insurance to two and a half million dollars, and the payout was double if he was murdered. I also made sure that the policy didn't have a suicide clause, just in case. *For the kids*, I told him, when he asked why we needed so much. He agreed and signed the papers, not realizing that he'd just signed his death warrant. Idiot. Five million dollars was more than enough to start a new life in Costa Rica.

I move away from the window and sit on a barstool at the counter. I am trying to figure out where my plan had gone wrong. After Claire had given me her phone number, I went to work. I sent her a couple of text messages, pretending to look for Brent. All I'd wanted was to make sure that she'd given me her real phone number. Once I verified that it was, I set up an account with one of those text messaging apps the kids are always using. It was easy. I had her real phone number and address, and I created an email account so that I could verify the app.

Over the next three months, I used the app to send myself several text messages. They were suggestive, dirty even. I would respond to them as if I were disgusted, horrified. When I thought I had enough "evidence," I printed them out and took them to the police station. The officer on duty, Greg Majors, was an old friend from high school, and I'd heard that his wife had left him for a woman. Perfect. When I said that the dirty lesbian next door was stalking me and threatening to hurt me if I didn't leave Brent, he responded by making out a report for harassment, and he assured me that she would be arrested that very day. He hated dykes just as much as I did. Brent was already dead, so all I had to do was move the body to a place where it could be found and the bitch would be the prime suspect.

So why isn't she still in jail? The first part of my plan had worked perfectly, but if she is out of jail, that might mean that they'll start looking at other suspects, and eventually they'll start looking at me. I do not intend to spend one minute in prison for killing the village idiot. Time to execute Plan B.

***

"Brent Powers is dead? How?" I am still in shock, and although I'm not yet sure how this is related to my arrest, I have a strange feeling that I'll soon find out. Reese and I have retired to our bedroom, and we are sitting on the loveseat in our pajamas drinking pear martinis, my favorite. I need something a little stronger than tea to get through the rest of this night. I know that Reese is still upset, but she is no longer mad at *me*, and that is all that matters right now.

"Yep. They found his body early this morning, just down the road really, over by the stables. He'd been shot five times in the chest at close range. Whoever did this wanted to make sure that he was dead," Reese says calmly.

"Who do you think did it?" I feel the panic rising again. I know that I didn't do it, but based on the events of the past 24 hours, I know that the police will come looking for me soon. I can't go to jail for something I didn't do, can I? *Oh, my God*, I thought to myself. *Of course I can.*

"Tia." Reese seems sure of herself, and I don't trust anyone in the world more than I trusted my Reese. Still, I have questions.

"How do you know?" I sit my drink on the console table, afraid that I'll spill it, my hands are shaking so badly.

Reese sits hers down too, and takes my hand in hers when she turns to face me.

"Claire," she says gently, "Tia set you up."

"What do you mean, 'set me up'? How? No way." I want to believe Reese, but how can what she's saying be true?

"Didn't you find it odd that she never messaged you after that second time? That she sent *you* a message looking for her husband when her sister lived right down the street?"

"Yes," I say. "But it wasn't a big deal. Maybe her sister wasn't home that night."

"Come on, Claire. Do you really think that? Why is this stranger asking you to check on her husband? I knew something was up the minute you told me that."

"Well, why didn't you stop me?"

Reese gives me a look.

"I tried, remember?" she says with only a touch of sarcasm in her voice. I really admire her restraint.

"Oh, yeah." I feel like a fool. Reese told me to ignore her messages, that no good would come from getting involved in whatever drama she had going on, and she had been right. Isn't she always? "But what does this have to do with the murder?" I'm a little tired, and I need Reese to connect the dots for me.

"Well, I've been doing a little digging. I found out that Brent had filed for bankruptcy a few weeks ago; it seems as though he had a gambling problem and was flat broke. I also discovered that Tia took out a large life insurance policy on him a few years ago. I think she'd had enough, and was just waiting for the right moment to get rid of him."

"Wait a minute, you really think she killed him for the life insurance? How do you know all of this?"

"Claire, I'm a glorified computer hacker, remember? I'm a forensic accountant, with a background in computer technology. What *can't* I find out?"

"Wow." I am dumbfounded, and quite impressed.

"I also learned that she's the one who reported you for stalking. But I found that out when I went to see you in jail. She claimed that you'd been texting her all kinds of nasty messages, and threatening to hurt her husband if she didn't leave him for you. You don't need a rocket scientist to figure out that she wanted the police to think that you had killed her husband."

"What? The only time I texted her was when she texted me first! And I didn't even know he was dead until you told me!" I am indignant; I cannot believe Tia would make up such lies about me. She isn't even my type. And setting me up for *murder*, I can't even look at dead animals on the side of the road without getting teary-eyed! On more than one occasion I've almost wrecked my car trying to avoid the squirrels that live on our street. I could never kill an actual person.

"Don't worry, I never believed that. But the police did, until I showed them your actual phone records this morning. It seems that she used your old phone number to sign up on a texting app. When I told them that you had your number changed a few weeks after we moved in, and showed them the records from the phone company, they agreed to do a little more digging. I'd already started, and showed them that she had used her own computer to create the account. Not smart. All they had to do was cross check the IP address to see that it wasn't you that was sending the messages. She never realized that your number wasn't active anymore, because she never tried to text you again, she was just texting herself through the app."

"They did all that last night?" I am baffled. On television this kind of thing takes forever. And our tiny police department is not that sophisticated.

"Nah. I helped them out a little, and I started looking right after you got that last text message. I just had no idea what I'd find, or that her husband would end up dead. I just knew that she was trouble. I gave everything else I found to Dara, and she'll give it to the prosecutor. Tia was smart, but not smart enough to use someone else's computer to create the dummy account. It's why they let you out of jail. Don't think for a minute that they wouldn't have kept you if I hadn't come back with those phone records and an attorney."

I don't know what to say; I am overwhelmed with information that my neighbor, a woman I'd intended to befriend, tried to set me up for murdering her husband, a man that I had never met. I know that it was still speculation at this point, but I have no doubt that Reese is right. I throw my arms around Reese and she holds me tight. Her tendency to overthink everything usually drives me crazy, but this time, I'm so glad that she did.

Reese's ringing cell phone startles us out of our embrace. She answers it and I take a sip of my tepid martini.

"It's over babe," Reese says, with a huge smile on her face.

"What?" I'm confused, which seems to be my mental state lately.

"That was Dara, they've dropped all of the charges against you."

"Oh, my God, really? It's over?" I start screaming with joy, and Reese picks me up and spins me around. We fall on the bed, exhausted, physically and mentally. It's over.

***

I've got to get the hell out of town. Plan B is simple: get the money and run. The kids are at my sister's house, and I'll send for them later. No time to waste. I've got to lay low until I get a copy of the death certificate, then it should be only a few days until I get my money. Just when I grab my suitcase, I hear the doorbell ring. I'm upstairs, so I look out of the window to see who it is before going down. It's the cops, and there's a bunch of them. That can only mean one thing. Dammit, this wasn't part of the plan. On to Plan C.

I walk into the closet and rumble around amongst the boxes of shoes. I've hidden it well, but I know it's in here. I find the box; it also holds a pair of black Via Spiga pumps from the old days. Back when I had dreams of having a shoe closet the size of my living room, back before Brent ruined it all. I pull out the nine-millimeter Glock, the same one I shot Brent with, and marvel at its lightness. Guns are supposed to be heavy. The officers are growing impatient; now they're banging on the door. I say a quick prayer for my children and put the barrel of the gun in my mouth. I've only got one shot, literally, and I have to do this right. I said that I did not intend to spend one second in prison for killing Brent, and that's exactly what I meant.

CATFISHED

I rifle through my tiny closet, trying to find the perfect outfit for tonight's date. Black leather mini-skirt and thigh-hi boots? Nope, too punk. Cardigan, pencil skirt, and pearls? Nah, too schoolteacher. Jeans and a cami? That felt right. I could add fringed booties and a leather jacket and it could work. Whew, now that that was out of the way, let me tell you about this date:

I've been talking to Peyton online for thirty days, and we are finally meeting up. Peyton seems perfect for me: intelligent, good sense of humor, and of course, drop-dead gorgeous. Their profile says they are six-three, (everyone always lies about their height), and they have a fluffy afro and piercing dark eyes. Eyebrows that look like fuzzy caterpillars and the kind of eyelashes you only see on babies. Perfect white teeth (probably capped) and brown skin that looks like a gift from the Caribbean gods. They are almost TOO good-looking, which makes me super suspicious. Did they steal a photo of Daveed

Diggs and use it on their profile? Because they could be twins. TWINS I tell you. Am I being catfished? It's hard to believe that I've met the perfect person on an online dating website. That only happens to white people in those ridiculous rom-coms, right? Right.

Regardless, I have always been partial to model-types, but that usually gets me into trouble, given their big egos and short attention spans. What? You know it's true. But Peyton seems different, they are thoughtful and attentive, and seem genuinely interested in everything I have to say. They even laugh at my blerd jokes. There is another reason that I'm apprehensive about tonight's date: I haven't been totally honest with Peyton about who I really am. Oh, I know I'm a hottie, smart too; but I've left out a couple of key details in my first email to Peyton. I mean, does anybody ever tell the whole truth about themselves on a dating site? I think not! I know you are dying to know what I said, so here's what I wrote:

> Hi Peyton,
> It seems we have a couple of things in common, and I'd love to chat with you about your love of Octavia Butler and Anne Rice. I'm also an old movie buff, so if you'd like to go to the Oldies But Goodies Film Festival next month let me know.
> A little more about me: I'm 27, single, and work as a librarian at the community college. I've been an out lesbian for the past ten years, and I'm just looking to get

to know some people since I'm pretty new to the area, but I'm definitely open to dating the right one. I hope to hear from you soon!
Jada

I was surprised when Peyton emailed me back within the hour, and we exchanged numbers soon after that. We've been talking on the phone for the past several weeks, and finally found a time to meet up.

I know that Peyton likes me, well, as much as you can like someone you haven't met in person, but I am still afraid that they'll run when they find out the truth. I generally don't tell my dates about my penchant for blood right away, and then it's often too late. Either they don't believe me and I have to give them a demonstration, (that usually doesn't end well), or they threaten to tell the authorities, (Um, who are they gonna tell, Count Dracula? Dude's been ash for quite a while now), and then I have to kill them. Most folks are aware that vampires are in the city, and some are even okay with it. But there are those who want to see us eradicated from the earth, so I've learned to be careful.

Needless to say, I don't date much.

So, tonight is either gonna be a clustercuss of fear and dread, or maybe, just maybe, Peyton could be the one. You know, the one I turn into a vampire and we live happily ever after, feeding on the blood of criminals and other unsavory types, because you know, we're ethical vampires and we don't REALLY want to hurt people, but we gotta eat too, ya know. Nah. I'm just kidding. I'm not really interested in turning anyone into a vampire. And being ethical can be a bit of a bore, but hey, I'm trying my best. More than anything, I just want to get my rocks off without a whole lot of drama. Maybe have someone to hang out with every now and then. See a show, the latest Jordan Peele movie or something. In other words, this Black girl just wants to have some fun.

***

Maaaan. This date with Jada tonight has been stressing me out. My crew told me to chill, but I don't know. What if she doesn't like me? I mean, I really shouldn't care, I *am* a model and can have any woman I want, but I want this one. Physically, she's just my type: about five-two (short people always lie about their height, so she's probably only five feet), dark brown skin, big ass afro, pretty eyes and teeth, and cleavage for days. Sweet baby jezuz, the cleavage. I could lose myself in those things. I almost asked her to send me a tit pic, but I didn't want to come off as a creep, but hey, I like what I like. And I like boobs. What? You know you do too!

She asked me to meet her at the pier, and my friend Gina told me that was just girl code for "I don't want to be alone with you yet." I ain't mad. I'd think I was a fake too. Women always look at my profile and think it's fake. It's not, it's really me. I can't help that I look like a Black Adonis. Blame my parents and their good genes. I'm just using them to my advantage. You meet a lot of good-looking women when you're a model, but most of them are high on heroin or so stuck-up that it's not worth the effort. Online dating is cool, but so many of these chicks online are fake, or married, or have three or four kids they *forgot* to mention, but want you to buy Pampers for. Nope, I don't want to be anybody's stepparent.

So, what to wear tonight? Black leather jacket, white tee, and jeans? Scratch that, I look like the Fonz. Blazer and button down? Too Wall Street. Khakis and a polo? Definitely not, too Carlton Banks. Black turtleneck and jeans it is. I know, I know. Isn't that what male models always wear? Yep, and you know why? Because it works. Shows off these chiseled cheeks and these eight-pack abs. I'll throw on a leather jacket to add a little pizazz. Yeah, kinda like Shaft, or Morpheus. Chicks dig those cats, don't they?

I didn't want to tell my crew, (which is why I'm talking to *you*), but I really think I like this one, well, as much as you can like someone you've only met online. But for real though, she's smart and sweet, the kind of girl I'd take home to mom. Well, if mom were speaking to me. Can you keep a secret? Sorry, sorry! I know you can, I just need to be sure. I know I told you that I got my good looks from my parents and that's true, but what I didn't say is that I haven't seen them in years. We kind of fell out about a family issue. They wanted me to join the family business and I said no. They said I was disloyal and stuff, threatened to take away my inheritance. To be honest, I was surprised. They didn't blink an eye when I came out as non-binary. Had no problem when I changed my name from Patricia to Peyton, but they had a fit when I told them I didn't want to hunt vampires for a living, that I didn't want to complete the ritual that would make me immortal. I mean, who wants to live forever anyway? Watching all your friends die, never getting married or having kids (not that I wanted any, but that's not the point). Anyway, I was like, cool, I can make a life for myself. I don't need your money. When I turned sixteen I moved out and got a job in New York. I've been doing just fine too, thank you very much. But last week, my sister Reva called and said they needed me back home. That there was a new threat in town and that they needed all the help they could get to take it down. That mom and dad were thinking about retiring and I need to start thinking about my place in the family. I told her I'd call her back later. But between me and you, I'm not calling her back. I like my life just the way it is, thank you very much, and there's nothing they can do to make me give it up.

***

So, Peyton is already ten minutes late, way to make an impression. I'm going to give them five more minutes and then I'm going back home. I might make a little pit stop at the pet store on the way. Don't look at me like that! I don't feel like hunting tonight, and you know that rejection always makes me feel some kinda way. I sit at my little table and people watch for a few more minutes, trying not to look at my cell phone. I really love it down here near the water, especially right as the sun goes down, and not because I'm a vampire either. It is peaceful and serene, even when it's crowded. I've never been in the water, but I love the sound of the ocean and of the seagulls calling to each other. Reminds me that life on earth isn't all bad.

Wait, is that them? Good lawd, they are *fine*! I really didn't believe the photos were real, but here they are, I guess I'd better get up and let them know I'm here.

"Peyton? Hey, I'm Jada. Nice to finally meet you in person." I'm still peeved that they are late so I offer my hand, but step back when they come in for a hug.

"Hey, Jada, good to see you! I've been walking around for ten minutes, this place is crazy. I haven't been down here in years and I got lost. Thanks for waiting," Peyton says, giving me a huge smile.

"It's okay." I smile back (it's really not, but I don't want to be an ass on our first date, also, *fine* covers a multitude of sins).

"Wanna grab a coffee or something? It's hard to talk out here with all of these people running around."

"Sure, a drink would be nice. One of my favorite bars is down here, and it shouldn't be too crowded now." I really want a bucket of blood, but vodka would have to do for the moment. Peyton seems nice so far, appropriately contrite at being late, and handsome enough for me to overlook it anyway. If nothing else, I'd get my flirt on, grab a bite, go home, and be no worse for the wear. If things go well, and I mean really well, I might invite them back to my place. What? You know it's been forever. I can do without your judgment thank you very much.

We walk the three blocks to the bar with Peyton chatting me up the entire way, man they can *talk*! They asked me about my job, my family, what kind of car I drove, (no car, who drives these days?), where I went to school, my favorite food, everything. I figured they'd be talked out by the time we got our drinks, and I was already starting to lose interest when they said something that got my attention.

"….Yeah, my folks want me to join the family business, but I'm not into it. Who wants to live in a rundown castle in the mountains? Not me."

"Your family has a castle?" I am intrigued. People have big houses, mansions even, but nobody lives in a *castle*.

"Yep, up in the hills, you know, it's about sixty miles from here, I haven't been home in years though. My folks cut me off when I told them I didn't want to be heir to the family throne." Peyton rolls their eyes in exasperation.

"What kind of business does your family have?" The hairs on my arms were starting to tingle, there were only a few kinds of people that lived in castles, and I don't want anything to do with any of them. Also, I've heard that a family of hunters was in the area, but Peyton can't be related to them, can they?

We decide to sit at the bar and choose a couple of stools down near the end where it's quiet. Peyton makes a great show of asking the bartender for recommendations, but eventually settles on a light beer. I thought my eyes would pop out of my head I rolled them so hard, but then I remember that they are a model, which again causes me to question what the heck I am doing on this date. I order my usual Moscow Mule, and turn to Peyton. I need to know more about this castle.

"So, you were about to tell me what kind of business your family is into."

"Was I? I guess I was. They're into import and export, I really don't know much about the details, just that I don't want to do it."

"Importing and exporting what? Surely you know that much." I press them on the details because I really need to know more about this Black family who lived in a castle in the foothills of the Cascade mountains. I mean, who *are* these people?

"I told you I'm not sure. All I know is that my grandparents settled here after moving down from Canada, and built their business. Some old white guy left my granddad the castle, which is why it's in our family. I guess if I paid more attention to family stories I'd know more details. Also, I left home at sixteen, which is around the time I would have starting learning more about my *place* in the family."

"Hmmmm." I don't believe a word coming out of their pretty mouth, but decide to let it go for now. I sat sipping my drink and thinking about how hungry I was. Maybe I should get a burger or something because I was starting to imagine my teeth in Peyton's neck.

***

Jada is staring off into space and fiddling with her napkin, which is making me nervous, so I decide to take a quick break to get myself together.

"Hey, Jada, I'm going to run to the restroom. I'll be right back, okay?"

"Sure. I'll be right here." Jada looks up gives me a wink as I walk off.

I walk in the bathroom, stand in front of the mirror, and grip the sides of the porcelain sink.

"Shit shit shit!" I know I'm talking too much, but I just can't help it. My sister Reva used to tell me that I suffered from diarrhea of the mouth. "Peyton," she used to say, "one of these days your mouth is going to write a check your body can't cash." She's probably right, but I just want to tell Jada *everything* about me. And I want to know everything about her too! She's prettier than her profile photos, I can tell she's really smart, and she didn't give me too much grief about being late for our date. I really did get lost. I don't come down here much, but I should have left earlier. And the boobs. The boobs are even better in person. You'd think I didn't have a pair the way I've been going on about them, but come on. You know the chicks I work with don't have much up top, and mine aren't anything to write home about either. Most days I don't even wear a sports bra. Jada's boobs look perfect. At least what I can see of them. That lil' cami she has on is giving me cleavage for days, and I'm having a hard time keeping my eyes on her face. Look, don't judge me; some folks love ass, I love boobs.

"Okay, okay. Take a deep breath, Peyton, you've got this; time to get back out there." My therapist taught me about self-talk and it really works. This date is just getting started and I don't want to mess it up. I've decided I'm going to tell her whatever she wants to know about me, including the stuff about my family. I don't want to start a new relationship with a lie, so I'll tell her the truth. It will be fine; I just know it.

***

I look up and see Peyton heading back toward the bar. They really are gorgeous, but I can't think about anything but the deep rumble in my belly.

"Hey, a table just opened up over there, wanna grab it? I'm hungry." I gesture to a booth over near the back of the bar. The place only has a few booths for food, but the burgers are really good, and I need meat. Rare. Now.

"Okay." Peyton stops abruptly and turns around, nearly knocking over a couple that is just about to sit down.

I pick up my drink and make my way to the table, smiling an apology at the couple Peyton had nearly hit. They scowl at me and take their place in line at the bar, which is now starting to fill up.

"This is great! Now we can really talk," Peyton says.

I have to stop myself from rolling my eyes; the only thing I want to know more about is this castle, but I have to figure out how to get what I want from them without being too obvious about it. Well, I know several ways I can get the information, but I really don't like pulling the vampire card unless I have to. Why not? You know why not. Because hypnotizing people without their consent isn't cool. And, yes, I know that taking their blood isn't either, but that's for survival, and a girl's gotta eat. Burgers can only take me so far.

"So, tell me more about your work?" Peyton really seems interested in knowing everything about me, but I am pretty sure we've covered some of this stuff in our phone conversations.

"What else do you want to know? I told you I'm a librarian at the community college. I work mostly in outreach, trying to create programs to get folks in the library. It's fun, and I get to actually talk to people sometimes." I am telling the truth about that. I really do enjoy my job, and it also gives me access to information, lots of information. As a librarian, I know how to find stuff most people don't even know exists, like old property deeds, business filings, and such. If Peyton won't tell me what I want to know about their family, I'll find out on my own.

The waitress comes up and I order my burger. Peyton orders a salad (dressing on the side) and a bottle of Perrier. Good grief they are a walking stereotype.

"Are you really going to eat your burger rare?" Peyton asks as the waitress walks away.

"Are you really going to eat a dry salad?" I snap back. I really should have eaten before walking down to the pier. I am *really* hungry, and it is starting to show.

"Sorry! I'm not trying to upset you; most women I know don't eat raw meat."

"I'm not most women."

"Well, I can see that! You're definitely different from most of the women I've dated," Peyton offers.

"How so?" I really don't care, but need to get my mind off of Peyton's carotid artery. I can hear their blood gurgling as it courses down to their heart. I turn to look out the window to distract myself.

"Well, for one, you're smart. Most of the models I know are pretty dense."

I raise my left eyebrow.

"I mean, they're model smart, but not book smart? You know what I mean." Peyton is digging a hole big enough to bury themself in.

"No, I really don't. What *do* you mean?" I am starting to think I've been Cyrano de Bergerac'd. I mean, this can't be the person I've been talking to on the phone for the past month. That person was sweet, thoughtful, and had never said anything sexist or misogynistic. *This* Peyton was turning into a Class A douchebag.

"Well, they're really good at their jobs, but don't know how to talk about anything other than diets or clothes or makeup," Peyton says.

"Hmmm. Well, most folks talk about work; theirs just happens to be about clothes, staying thin, and makeup. I don't see anything wrong with that." I'm not going to let them off the hook that easily.

"Maybe you're right. Oh, and I know how else you're different!" Peyton's eyes light up.

"Oh, yeah?" I gulp down the rest of my drink. I really want another one, but am afraid I won't be able to control the urge to sink my teeth into Peyton's neck. I *really* should have eaten something before coming down here today.

"You have a really nice body! Most of the girls, um women I know are so thin you can see their ribcages. It's not attractive at all. They're too skinny for me. You have, um, nice curves." Peyton looks directly at my chest, not hiding a smile.

Glub glub. Glub glub.

It has only been five minutes since I placed my order, and this place is notoriously slow when it comes to food. I'm not going to make it. I am also starting to think that this date had been a mistake.

"Peyton. Peyton!" I nearly had to yell to get their attention, they were so busy telling me how much they loved my Afro, my nail polish, (I loved blood red nail polish), my boots, my leather jacket, literally every single thing about me that they could see, and probably some they'd made up.

"Huh? Oh, I'm sorry. I guess I was getting a little carried away."

I figure this is my opportunity to learn more about Peyton's family.

"I think you know much more about me than I do about you. Tell me more about your family. What are they like? You said they live in a castle? I'd love to hear more about that." I shift my body so that my thigh touches theirs under the table. Whoops, bad idea, now I can feel their femoral artery. I move it back.

"Well, I kinda didn't tell the truth earlier." Peyton looks sheepish.

"Hmmm. Which part? The import or the export?" I know they haven't been telling me the truth, but I didn't know they'd come clean this quickly. I'm not sure if this is a good or bad sign.

"Well, it's not so much a lie as not the whole truth."

"Go on." I am trying to be patient. And I am hungry. *Glub glub. Glub glub.*

"My family *is* in the import/export business, but that's not all they do."

"What else do they do?" Good gracious this was like pulling teeth. One minute they're running off at the mouth and now it's like they've lost all of their words.

"Um. Well, you're not gonna believe this, but they hunt vampires."

"They do what?" I hear them the first time, but need a moment to collect myself. In an instant my body has gone from relatively relaxed to survival mode, and I am afraid that I won't be able to control the urge to snatch their throat out of their neck, right there at the table. I also need to know more.

"They hunt vampires. That's the family business that I told you about. I left home at sixteen, before I could start my training. Who wants to hunt vampires? I sure don't." Peyton was actually pouting, and if the situation wasn't so serious, I would have giggled at the look on their face.

"Hmmm," I said, trying to keep my emotions at bay.

"My family has been hunting vampires for centuries, and my parents are ready to retire. My sister called me up and told me that my folks want me to come home. I told her I wasn't going to do it and that they couldn't make me." Peyton almost looks pleased with themself, it's comical, really.

Like I mentioned earlier, everyone knows that vampires are in the city, right along with fairies and werewolves, (although they mostly live on the East Coast), and other fantastical beings, but most folks leave us alone. Those of us that need blood to survive have found new and creative ways to feed, so the authorities ignore us or pretend that we don't exist. And of course, there are always groupies, mostly pale-skinned women wanting to be seduced by a vampire. Gurl, bye. Seduction is for romance novels and Marlene Dietrich; vampires, like most people, are looking for reciprocity in relationships.

Which brings me to my current problem.

I can keep pretending that I'm human and let this little scenario play itself out, finding one reason or another to ghost them (no pun intended) after a couple of dates. But what if Peyton is lying about their relationship with their family? What if they already know what I am? *What if this whole date is a setup?* A part of me doesn't believe that, Peyton doesn't seem to harbor any malice toward vampires, but I haven't lived for some three-hundred odd years by taking unnecessary risks.

"Wanna get out of here?" I ask softly.

"What about your burger? I thought you were starving?" Peyton looks genuinely concerned, and for a minute, I almost change my mind.

Glub glub. Glub glub.

"Come on, let's go. I live only about three blocks from here." I throw a twenty-dollar bill down on the table, grab their hand and lead them out of the bar.

Glub glub. Glub glub.

The pounding in my ears is getting louder. We have to get away from the throngs of people walking near the pier. It's even more crowded than it was when I arrived earlier that evening. People love to come to the pier at night, mostly to drink and hook-up, which, coincidentally, is exactly what I had been planning to do, too. I see a deserted alley about a block away and steer Peyton toward it. I'm pretty sure they think they're going to get their hands on these 38DDs tonight.

Glub glub. Glub glub. Glub glub.

I check behind me as we turn into the alley to make sure that no one sees us. There's a woman cooking collard greens with smoked turkey in the apartment three floors up, and a baby with a dirty diaper on the first floor. His mom is still breastfeeding and she's leaking through her shirt. At this point, my need to feed is so strong that I can't control any of my senses and I'm being bombarded with everything at once.

I push Peyton against the brick of the building and press my body against theirs. They smell like lavender soap, Armani, and oil sheen, because what Black model doesn't?

"Oh, so you want it right here? This is hot, I knew that you were turned on, I could tell by how you were looking at me, but I thought we'd wait until we got to your place. This is fine, although it's a little dirty." Peyton turns their nose up at the trash on the ground, although it isn't much, just a few bottles and old newspapers.

Glub glub. Glub glub. Glub glub.

"Yes, I want it right here." My eyes are glued to the left side of their neck, which I can see pulsing under their turtleneck. I take their face in my hands and give them a long hard kiss on the lips, hooking my fingernails under the fold in their shirt. In my boots, we are about the same height, so I have no trouble reaching their neck. Peyton puts their arms around my waist, hands resting lightly on my butt, which is perfect, I don't want them to fall when I am finished.

I nuzzle Peyton's neck and gently pull the turtleneck down, kissing them lightly, as I expose more of their flesh. Peyton groans softly and pulls me closer.

Glubglubglubglubglubglub.

Finally, I sink my teeth into Peyton's neck and drink. I felt their body stiffen as they realize what I am doing. They try to pull away, but I hold tight.

"Wait, what are you doing? Are you *biting* me? What the hell is going on? OMG you're a vampire? Reva is going to kill me!" I hold fast, quite sure that Reva isn't going to kill them. Peyton struggles to get away, but of course I am too strong. Like I said, I only use my powers when it's absolutely necessary, and right now, it is necessary.

I drink until I am full, listen carefully to make sure that no one is around, and gently ease Peyton's lifeless body into the dumpster at the end of the alley. I lick my lips to make sure there isn't any blood on them, fluff my Afro, straighten my jacket, and walk back up the pier and toward home.

What? I told you I don't date much.

PROJECT M

Teagan stared out of the window and looked down at the glistening city below her. Atlanta was an old city, but not as old as the newly deserted New York. Over the past two hundred years, Atlanta had become the economic and cultural center of this half of the continent. It was remarkable, because Teagan had read in the old history books that people had hated what was then known as the South; they'd thought it backwards, slow, and undeniably racist. Now, it was the most technologically advanced region in the world, as well as the most diverse. Atlantans had divested from fossil fuels back around 2150 and rebuilt the city's transportation system; streamlined its airport, and welcomed the use of advanced technology when other cities were still trying to figure out who owned the rights. They had also protected and nourished their green spaces, so this region now had the best air quality of a hemi-city its size, now nearly twenty million souls. She often wondered what the area had been like before the hover-rail that served as the hemi's main mode of transportation, or the shuttles that whisked folks off to other parts of the world from the airport, reaching most destinations in under three hours. Some folks still used indie pods, but they were clunky and unpredictable, really only built for short trips, like the open air markets that sat atop most apartment buildings. Just last month one had crashed into a building after it had been in the air for over two hours, more than four times its recommended flight time.

Teagan couldn't help but notice what a beautiful day it was: the sky was as blue as it ever gets, and there wasn't a cloud in sight. A perfect day for a funeral. She turned and walked back toward her living area and thought about the day's events. The woman who had raised her from birth, Noe, had been cremated earlier that morning. Noe hadn't wanted a fuss, so there'd only been a few people at the funeral: Teagan's godmother Miranda Li, a couple of Noe's close colleagues, and the priest, an old family friend. After the service, everyone had gone their separate ways. It was almost as if it hadn't happened at all.

Teagan had mixed feelings about the whole thing. Of course she was upset that the only mother she'd ever known was gone, but she'd always had questions about her birth mother, Taryn. Noe never tried to hide the fact that she hadn't given birth to Teagan, but she'd never told her what had happened to the woman who had carried her in her belly for nearly nine months. All Teagan knew was that she'd died giving birth to her. Teagan had always found that hard to believe, (who dies in childbirth these days?), but until a few days ago, she'd accepted it as truth. Now, she wasn't so sure. Teagan pressed the call button for

Max to bring her a fruit tonic, and thought about what she had learned over the past few days.

It had been an accident, really. Not long after Noe died, Teagan had been going through her files, trying to locate an insurance policy. Teagan didn't need the money, but that wasn't the point, she still had to file the paperwork. She was surprised that folks still kept track of family estates in this day and age; who really cares what you leave your kids or partner? But governments will be governments, all bureaucracy and no common sense. Also, they wanted to get their cut. Noe wasn't a member of the uber-rich, but she'd been well-off, and Teagan knew that there'd be taxes to pay, especially on the royalties from some of her patents. Noe kept meticulous records, so the computer file containing the policy shouldn't have been hard to find. There were files for medical records, the android's service records, the deed to the condo, even scanned copies of receipts for office supplies from twenty years ago. But no insurance policy. She knew that one existed, she'd heard Noe talking about it with Miranda during her final days in hospice. She hadn't paid much attention then, figuring it would be filed away on her computer like everything else, but now, she couldn't find it. Then a few days later, she'd clicked a file named "Luna 6000," really because at this point, she figured that Noe had somehow misfiled it and she'd just have to go through all of the files with insurance as a tag. She'd almost closed the file as quickly as she'd opened it, because it was just an insurance policy on an old smart device. Teagan had heard about it, but the technology had been outdated for quite a while, and nearly everyone, including the city itself, now used the Jupiter X for everything from v-chatting with friends to scooting around in their shuttles. Only a few people still actually owned cars, (mostly folks who didn't trust shuttles), but they all relied on the Jupe's technology to get them where they needed to go. But Teagan had seen her mother's name attached to this Luna 6000, so she'd continued to read. Her mother had bonded with a Luna 6000 while she was pregnant with Teagan, and it had somehow malfunctioned and killed her. But that wasn't what Noe had told her. She'd never mentioned a smart device in connection with her mother's death. And why wouldn't she? And what ever happened to the Luna 6000 that had killed Taryn? If she could locate it, maybe it would provide some answers. Teagan had printed the file and showed it to Miranda, asking her what she knew about it.

"Why would you want to go digging up all that old stuff?" Miranda had asked.

"Why not? Noe never explained exactly how my mother died, and I want to know what happened. I've kept these questions to myself for most of my life, not wanting to hurt Noe's feelings. But now that she's gone, I think I deserve to know."

Miranda's normally rosy cheeks had paled, and she wouldn't look Teagan in the face. At first Teagan didn't understand why, but then it dawned on her that Miranda probably knew the truth. After all, she'd been Noe's best friend, and the two women had been extremely close. They'd pretty much raised Teagan together, and Teagan thought of her as a third mother. Of course she knew what had happened to Taryn. She'd performed the Cesarean section that had delivered her twenty-five years ago. Teagan kicked herself for not thinking about it before, but it didn't make sense that the women would keep this from her. What were they hiding? Teagan initially felt a bit of guilt for thinking that her moms might be hiding something; after all, neither of the women were related to her by blood, but then she realized that she had every right to know what happened to Taryn, even though she'd never met her. Taryn was the woman who had given her life.

Max's arrival with the tonic snapped Teagan back into the present moment.

"Would you like anything else, Lady Teagan?"

"No, Max. Thank you." Teagan stifled a giggle at Max's formality. It must have been hardwired into his system. Max turned to go and it occurred to her that Max had also been present the night of her birth. Max had been Taryn's android, and Noe refused to replace him, even though there were dozens of newer models on the market. She'd always believed that Noe kept him around because he reminded her of the time before Taryn's death, but maybe that wasn't it at all. Max had been upgraded over the years, but he might still have data from that day in his memory banks. Now that she thought about it, there were probably years of information rattling around inside his head somewhere. The only question was how to get it.

"Max, wait."

"Yes, Lady?"

"What happens to your back-up data when you get an upgrade?"

"There's a file with all of my back-ups on the main hard drive in the house, Lady Teagan."

"Thanks, Max."

Max floated into the kitchen and Teagan knew that

she needed to see the back-ups from the year of her birth, 2227. Teagan sipped her beverage and decided she needed to clear her calendar for the weekend. She also knew just who to get to help her.

***

Teagan finished her drink (Max made the *best* fruit tonics) and walked over to her office. She stood at her desk and tapped twice on her Jupe X monitor to connect to her partner, Jayce. She knew that Jayce would help her sort through Max's old back-ups, even though she was sure that they'd disapprove.

"Hey, babe." Jayce looked up from their screen and blew Teagan a kiss. "How are you feeling?"

"I'm all right, I guess. It was a funeral. Funerals are always depressing, even when you see them coming."

"I know, babe."

"What are you doing this weekend?" Teagan figured she'd start with that. She already knew that Jayce would question her desire to dig up the past. Jayce didn't believe in looking backward, for any reason. It drove her crazy sometimes, but it was a small price to pay for the love of her life. She knew it had something to do with their family history, so most of the time, she just let it go. One day she'd get the story though, but it would not be today.

"Why?" Jayce was immediately suspicious. Teagan never asks what they're doing, so they knew something was up. Jayce stopped working on whatever it was that they were working on and gave Teagan their full attention.

"I want you to help me with something."

"Go on." Jayce's voice was soft, yet firm. Almost a command. Teagan loved it when they got all serious on her. It was kind of sexy.

"IwanttogothroughallofMax'soldback-upstoseeifIcan findoutwhathappenedtomybirthmomonthedayshedied." The words tumbled out of her mouth in one long stream, and once they were out, Teagan opened her eyes and took a deep breath. She hadn't realized that she had closed them or stopped breathing.

"You want to do what? What did you just say?" Jayce looked perplexed.

"I want to go through all of Max's old back-ups to see if I can find out what happened to my birth mom on the day she died."

"Teagan…" Jayce rolled their eyes and got that look on their face that Teagan alternately loved and hated.

"Jayce, listen. It's for a good reason. I don't think Noe told me the truth about my mother's death. I need to find out what she was hiding from me. I think something bad happened to her on the day she gave birth to me."

"Well, we know something bad happened, she died in childbirth. Why are you dredging up all of this old stuff? Let it be."

"Don't you think I have a right to know what happened to her?" Teagan was getting frustrated. Didn't they know that history mattered? That she had a right to know more about the origins of her birth?

Jayce looked at her for a minute and then got up and walked out of the room. Before Teagan could protest, they were back with a tiny keycard attached to a red lanyard.

"This will unlock the code to Max's main drive. Just insert the card into the android slot in the main panel and wait for the data to load on the house Jupe. It'll be faster than going through the individual files," Jayce said.

Teagan watched Jayce pull an envelope out of a drawer, drop the keycard in, seal it and insert it into the mail chute. It would arrive at Noe's condo in five minutes.

"Wait, how did you..." Teagan was dumbfounded.

"Um, I help design these condos and the systems that keep them running, remember? Also, I did Max's last back-up. When he had that system malfunction and Noe called me over to fix him? She gave me a copy of the keycard in case anything else happened and because she knew you'd call me anyway. There's a copy somewhere in Noe's house, or maybe Miranda's place, I'm not sure. So, don't lose this one. I'll be over at eight sharp to help you sort through the data."

"I love you, you know that?"

"Yeah, I know." Jayce smiled showing perfect white teeth, blew another kiss, and signed off.

***

Miranda Li spoke softly into her Jupe X and a nearby transport shuttle floated over to where she was standing on the curb. She hopped in and held her wrist against the screen for five seconds so that it could read her implant, and settled back in her seat for the trip home. As she sped away from her best friend's funeral, she thought about the secret that she'd kept for twenty-five years. She loved her goddaughter, but there was no way that she was going to let her find out that she and Noe had been responsible for her birth mother's death.

She arrived at her home and strode directly to her office/lab. She wasn't quite sure what Teagan thought she'd found, but she knew for sure what she didn't want her to find. She thought back to that night over two decades ago when she'd gotten the call from Noe that it was time to deliver Taryn's baby. Taryn never knew that she'd signed her death warrant the moment she decided to carry their child. Noe had grown disillusioned with the marriage some two years earlier, and when she'd mentioned divorce, Miranda had talked her out of it, realizing that they had been given a unique opportunity to see their research brought to life.

"You know, Taryn is a perfect candidate for our experiment." Miranda had broached the subject carefully. She knew that Taryn would have to die, but she wasn't sure that Noe fully understood the implications of their work.

"I think you're right. But what will we tell the baby? Or anybody else that asks?"

"We'll tell her that her mother died in childbirth. She won't know any different," said Miranda.

"Yeah, but she won't be stupid. Nobody dies in childbirth anymore. Every now and then a surrogate rejects a fetus, but they don't *die*." Noe was an obstetrician, and she'd never lost a patient in childbirth.

"As a matter of fact they do; and just because you've haven't lost any patients doesn't mean that none of them die. Women have and will always die in childbirth. But that doesn't matter. What matters is that you are okay with this. Taryn dying." There, she'd said it out loud, more for her own benefit than for Noe's.

"Yep. I'm okay with it. She was always window dressing. I'm a doctor, I needed a wife, and she was just as good as any woman in the hemi. I want a child, and I don't need her to have one, and if you think it'll be better if we use Taryn, I'm okay with that."

"Damn, Noe. Tell me how you really feel!" They both burst out laughing at that; Noe had been complaining about Taryn for years. The truth was that she should have never married her. Neither of these women ever cared much about love or romance, but Noe did care about keeping up appearances, thus her need for a wife. Miranda had no such need. She'd vowed to stay single the rest of her life. She had an android to take care of her physical needs.

"Then it's settled, I'll convince Taryn to connect to the Luna and we'll have about eight months to see if we can make a baby."

And exactly eight and a half months after implantation, Miranda received the message that it was time to deliver the baby. Everything had gone according to plan: the Luna had *malfunctioned* and caused Taryn's death, and Noe had assisted Miranda with the Caesarean section, even setting up a mock surgery unit in the basement of the home she'd shared with her now dead wife. Little Teagan was perfect in every way, well except one. There were only two people in the entire world, well, one now that Noe was dead, who knew that Teagan was only half human. Miranda was determined to make sure that it stayed that way.

***

As promised, Jayce showed up at Noe's condo at eight a.m. sharp, ready to help Teagan go through Max's old data. Jayce wanted this to be over; they were really ready for Teagan to move back into her own place and out of this condo. She'd stayed with Noe the last few weeks of her life, and they also wanted Teagan to put this so-called mystery to rest. Jayce agreed that something had always seemed off about Taryn's death, but they also believed in letting the past stay where it was. Anyway, what did it matter now? Taryn had been dead for twenty-five years, and now that Noe was dead, was it really all that important? Jayce wasn't all that sure that it was, but knew that they needed to support Teagan no matter what. They pressed the button to signal their arrival at the condo.

"Hey, baby!" Teagan greeted Jayce with a hug and kiss. Jayce stood there for a minute and enjoyed the feel of Teagan's body against theirs. It had been a long time since they'd been alone together, and they hadn't realized how much they'd missed the way the curve of Teagan's body fit perfectly with theirs.

Teagan broke the embrace after a few more seconds and led Jayce to the condo's control room. She'd already downloaded thirty years of Max's backups, but had no idea where to begin.

"Okay, I'll start with the year before your birth and we'll work forward from there. What did you do with the old Luna 6000 manual that you found?" Jayce didn't waste any time getting to work.

"It's in Noe's office. I'll go get it and have Max make you a cup of tea, okay?"

"Thanks, babe." Jayce pulled a chair up to the floating monitor and starting clicking through the files.

Teagan ran up the stairs to Noe's office to retrieve the manual, but knew immediately that it was gone as soon as she walked in. She'd left it on the left corner of the desk, and now it was missing.

"Max!"

"Yes, Lady Teagan?" Max appeared as if out of nowhere. She hated when he did that.

"Have you cleaned in here? I put something on the desk and now it's gone." Teagan shuffled a few papers on the desk, but she knew that the manual wasn't there.

"No ma'am. But perhaps I can locate it for you. What is it that you're looking for?"

Teagan paused for a minute, she wasn't sure that she should tell Max about the Luna or about what was going on. She decided to take her chances.

"It's an old manual. For the Luna 6000. My mom was connected to one when she died. I wanted to see if I could learn something about her death by looking through it."

"Oh, yes Lady Teagan. Dr. Li took it with her when she left yesterday. Will there be anything else?" Max waited patiently for her to respond.

"No. Thank you, Max."

Teagan felt faint and confused, so she sat down in Noe's old office chair. It was a deep burgundy leather, cracked and split on the seat and arms from years of use and neglect. The once shiny brass studs hadn't been polished in years, so they were now a dusty pecan color. When Teagan was younger, Noe liked to collect antique furniture; there were lots of strange pieces around the house, stuff from the time before even Noe's parents were born, she was sure of it. But Noe never took care of the things she worked so hard to find. All of them were in disrepair, or so old that they were falling apart. Like the grandfather clock from the nineteenth century with the broken glass panes and missing front leg. It was propped up on the wall on the other side of the office, dangerously close to falling over. It still worked though, and before Noe died, she'd dial it up and Teagan would watch the pendulum swing back and forth for hours, hypnotized. She stared at the clock now and felt a sense of calm descend over her body. After learning that Miranda had taken the manual, she'd almost passed out from what she initially thought was the onset of a panic attack. She now realized that she was just hungry.

"Max," she called out into the hallway beyond the office, "will you make me a sandwich?"

"Of course, Lady Teagan. What would you like?" Max appeared in the doorway before she could decide what she wanted.

"Surprise me." Max's face seemed to frown, but then his processors figured out what she meant and he hastened a smile. It never ceased to amaze her how much he looked and acted like a human. Did he have thoughts of his own, or was he only able to process commands?

He'd been upgraded several times over the years, and she wondered if it was time to replace him. Nah. Max was the only thing left that was connected to the time before her mother died. Well, except for Miranda, and Teagan was beginning to think that she didn't know the woman as well as she thought she had.

Teagan logged into Noe's computer to print out another copy of the Luna 6000's manual, only to discover that the file was missing. Now, Teagan was sure that Miranda had something to do with Taryn's death. No one else had access to the house or Noe's office. When Noe was diagnosed with an incurable blood disease, Teagan had given Miranda the updated entry codes so that she could come and go as she pleased; she'd always done so when she was a kid, but had stopped coming over as often when Teagan was around sixteen. She never figured out why Miranda didn't just live with them, she was always either at their house or at her lab.

Teagan clicked through a few more files to make sure that she hadn't overlooked the manual, but gave up after a few minutes. Her gut was telling her that Miranda had erased the files because she didn't want Teagan to find out the truth, which made her even more determined to figure it all out. Her instincts were telling her that something other than childbirth had killed her mother.

***

Miranda fiddled with the lock on her old gray metal file cabinet; most of the handles were broken but there was only one drawer she needed to open. Nobody used these old things anymore, and there probably wasn't another like it in the city, well, except for the identical one at Noe's place. Miranda choked back a sob as she rifled through the third drawer in search of the files that detailed her and Noe's work together. It was hard to believe that her best friend was gone. The women had had such high hopes when they started their work over thirty years ago. To be sure, Miranda was the brains behind the operation and while Noe was a doctor and extremely intelligent, she didn't have the patience for research, which is why she became a physician and not a scientist. She did, however, fund the venture that they eventually called Project M. Both women were interested in reproductive research, something that male scientists eschewed unless it involved new and exciting ways to extend human male erections. What Miranda wanted to do, what she believed was possible, was a way to create synthetic sperm, thus eliminating the need for men in the reproductive process.

Yes, sperm donation centers existed, (Miranda's friend owned Happy Family, which was how they were able to inject Taryn with Project M without her knowing that it wasn't *real* sperm), but women still relied on donations from men in order to have a baby. Women who used these centers sometimes paid tens of thousands of dollars for what they thought was *top* sperm, only to find out later that it was all a lie. There had even been a case in the mid-hemi (it was known as Indiana back then), where a doctor who performed the insemination procedure had used his own sperm and sired dozens of children, none of whom he actually helped to parent. Miranda wanted to give people more choice, especially lesbians like Noe, and the genderless like Jayce, who really didn't want to deal with an overly involved sperm donor. Women did not need men to raise children, why should they need them to create them?

And so they set out to create a viable sperm substitute, a substance that women could inject while in the privacy of their own homes and by means of a process where no human males were involved. It was rough going the first few years of research. Miranda sampled sperm from hundreds of living creatures trying to find one compatible with human female eggs. It took her exactly twelve years, but she was finally able to use a mixture of simian, fish, and synthetic products to create a sperm that would impregnate a female human egg, and create a viable embryo.

It was a bit of a joke between them really, naming it Project M after milt; the gravamen of Project M was proprietary, and neither simian nor fish, only trace portions of those creatures were actually in their synthetic sperm. Just enough to serve as a binding agent and to ensure upward movement in the vaginal canal. And finding eggs to experiment with wasn't as hard as one would think. Women had been selling their eggs for research and other use for hundreds of years. And while male scientists had never been able to figure out how to keep women from dying in childbirth, they'd figured out how to increase the number of eggs women passed every month from one to five. No one thought it possible, but leave it to the patriarchy to find more ways to impose compulsory motherhood on women. Now, the chances of multiple births increased exponentially; more eggs, more babies. It wasn't hard to see what they wanted to accomplish with that. Fewer women were having babies, but the ones that did tended to have more multiple births, decreasing the likelihood of them returning to the workplace or entering public service, that is if they actually wanted it. Of course, there were women who advocated for more egg production, why wouldn't there be? Just like there were women who were pro-birth but anti-sex education. Pro-forced sterilization of Black and Brown women, but anti-vasectomy for their white husbands and sons. Same shit, different century. Wasn't it ancient King Solomon who said that there was nothing new under the sun? Well, he wasn't wrong.

Tears welled up in her eyes as she thought about how successful they'd been. But how they'd never be able to share Project M with the women of the world. Yes, they'd been able to create a synthetic sperm that actually worked! But they'd also committed a cold-blooded murder in order to test it. Not only that, but the ethical questions associated with the child were myriad. The baby would be only half human. The rest was, well, Miranda wasn't sure. They'd watched Teagan grow up over the past 25 years and there were no external indications that she wasn't a fully human person.

But she wasn't. Even trace amounts of nonhuman substances corrupt human DNA, so they'd had to create something to counteract the effects of those, let's say idiosyncrasies. The only thing that they knew could work was A.I. Over the past few years scientists and engineers had developed A.I. so advanced that most androids were barely detectable from humans. Miranda was quite sure that there were more of them living as humans than most people wanted to admit. How else would scientists understand A.I. and human interactions if they weren't out there living and working among us? There was only so much one could do in a lab. Thus, the problem Miranda currently faced. Teagan wasn't fully human, but she could never know the real truth of her conception and birth. With her last breath Noe had made her promise that she wouldn't let their daughter find out that she wasn't fully human. Or that they'd killed her mother. Over the years, Noe had grown soft. She no longer cared about their research and had expressed regret over murdering Taryn. She also wanted to protect Teagan from the truth, and from becoming a lab rat if the world ever found out what she really was. For Miranda, part of her joy had been derived from working with her best friend, and now that Noe was gone, she no longer had the drive to continue her work. She wanted to retire in peace. The only other person that knew the truth was dead, and once she destroyed the files, she'd know that their secret was safe.

***

Max felt bad about lying to Teagan, (at least he *thought* he felt bad, his cognitive function was superb, but he wasn't too sure about feelings, even though his last upgrade came with a wide range of human emotions), but he didn't have a choice. Dr. Li hadn't taken the manual, Max had; he wanted to be sure that he'd remembered things correctly before sharing his suspicions with his new administrator. He didn't like that word very much (Max guessed he *did* have feelings), because Teagan was so much more than an administrator to him. He wanted to protect her, keep her from harm, be there when she needed him. Max guessed the word he was looking for was *family*. Yes, Teagan was family. He'd been there when she was born, and he suspected he'd be there when she died. Androids never died, they were upgraded until they were no longer compatible with the hardware and then they were decommissioned. Max was fortunate, all of his parts had been modernized about ten years ago, so he was just as good as any of the new models. With care, he'd be around another 300 years or so. Humans also had an extended life capacity, but most expired at around 200 years old or went into a cryostate, hoping that some new technology would come along and revive them. Even with all of the new advances in technology, science hadn't yet figured out how to bring humans back to life, which is why they were working so hard to live longer. And why they were now fusing human and android technologies. Max speculated that eventually, human and android would be indistinguishable. Ergo, his dilemma.

His previous administrator, Noe, had not been careful. Although Max had been designed to serve, to inhabit the shadows of human existence, it did not mean that he was unobservant. In fact, Max processed every bit of data that he came into contact with, that's what made him so efficient. It's also how he knew that Noe and Dr. Li had murdered Taryn, his original administrator, all those years ago. Not only that, but Jayce had figured out that Max's backup files would contain all of that data (that Jayce is a smart one, Max liked them very much), and now Max was faced with an ethical dilemma. It was his duty to serve and protect Teagan, and that meant from everything, including information that might hurt her. On the other hand, Teagan wanted, no *needed* to know what had happened to her mother. Wasn't Max duty bound to tell her? Max had searched his database and there was nothing in the index that covered this situation. He had not been programmed for this. However, this last backup had revealed something interesting. Max was thinking, no feeling, that he would have to decide for himself what to do, and it would need to be soon. Jayce was bound to discover the files that would prove that Dr. Li had tampered with the Luna 6000, causing it to malfunction and send Taryn into an early labor. They would also find out that Noe and Dr. Li had planned the whole thing, that sweet little Teagan had been an experiment, albeit a successful one. Finally, Teagan would find out that she and Max were more alike than she could ever imagine. Brother and sister really, family. He had failed in his duty to Taryn, but he would not fail her daughter. She deserved to know the truth.

Max put the finishing touches on Teagan's sandwich, ham and Swiss, just like Taryn used to eat, placed it and a glass of sweet iced tea on a silver tray, and floated into the office where Jayce and Teagan were poring over Max's old backups. Although Max could not sweat, he felt his processors speed up with what must have been nervousness.

"Pardon me, Lady Teagan. Might I have a word with you?" Max placed the tray and sandwich on a nearby desk, and stood erect with his hands behind his back.

"Oh, hey Max. What's up?" Teagan looked tired, even though it was only noon. It had been a long morning. She was sitting on the floor, surrounded by paper. Noe had liked to print things out to read them, even though most people used their screens. Teagan said it made her eyes hurt, (probably because she refused to wear her corrective lenses), so she read most long documents on paper too.

Jayce, ever efficient, was sitting at the desk reading another set of files directly from the floating screen. Max detected a change in Jayce's heart rate, and knew that it was time.

"Lady Teagan, Dr. Li did not take the manual, I did."

"What?" Teagan looked confused.

"I said Dr. Li…"

"No, stop, I heard you, I just don't understand. Why would you take the manual Max?" Teagan wasn't sure she wanted to hear what he had to say, but somehow knew that it had something to do with her mother's death.

"Because I was trying to protect you, Lady Teagan." Max was still nervous (if that was what he had been feeling), but also sure that he was doing the right thing.

"Protect me from what, Max?" Teagan's hands were sweating and she was starting to feel light-headed again.

"From the fact that Noe and Miranda killed your mother." Jayce was never one to beat around the bush. Teagan usually appreciated that in them, but this was one time where she wished Jayce would be a little less direct.

"What?" Teagan knew she was starting to sound like a broken record, but she didn't know what else to say. Although she had suspected that Noe had been hiding something from her, she really hadn't prepared herself for finding out what that was.

"I'm afraid Mx. Jayce is correct, Lady Teagan. While it's true that your birth mother did die in childbirth, they fabricated the glitch in the Luna 6000 that sent her into an early labor in order to force a Caesarean section. They then left her to bleed to death on the operating table. Your mother was not meant to survive the ordeal." Max bowed his head, contrite.

"Oh, my god. Are you sure? How do you know all of this?" Teagan's eyes welled up with tears, she had never known her birth mother, but the thought of her dying alone after giving birth filled her with a sadness she hadn't known was possible. Jayce had told her to leave the past alone, and now she wished she had listened to them.

"I was there, Lady Teagan. I was not in the room when Lady Taryn died, but I was nearby. My processors collected the data and stored it in my hard drive, but at that time, I was not able to act under my own cognitive power. I could not save her." Max could not cry, but he looked grieved.

"There's more." Jayce was squinting at the screen.

"Wait, don't you say a word." Teagan couldn't bear anymore of Jayce's bluntness. "Max, what else do you have to tell me?"

Max looked at Jayce as if for help, and they gave him a reassuring nod.

"Dr. Noe and Dr. Li were working together on something they called Project M. You are the result of their research." Max paused for a moment and Jayce picked up where Max left off.

"Project M is synthetic sperm, it's right here in the files. They injected it into your birth mom, and created you. A.I. filled in some of the molecular gaps in Project M, which means that you're part android? Is that even possible?" Jayce was stunned at this discovery; how could Noe and Miranda have done this? They hadn't taken the women for evil scientists, but that is what they were. The pair had murdered Teagan's mother in order to use her body for their experiment.

Teagan sat on the floor, stunned into silence. Did this mean she wasn't human? Of course she was, her mother was human, so that meant she was, too. But what about this other stuff, Project M? It was too much to process right now, she had to go lay down somewhere. No, first she needed to call Miranda Li and confront her.

Jayce saw Teagan trying to get up from the floor and knew immediately what she intended to do.

"Oh, no you don't! You can't call Miranda, Teagan. At least not now. Give yourself a little while to process, this is a lot." Jayce led Teagan over to the settee in the office and made her put her feet up. "Max, can you bring Lady Teagan a cold cloth for her head?"

"Of course, Mx. Jayce." Max floated off to get the towel.

"How could they, Jayce? I mean, I don't even care about the experiment part, I mean, aren't we all heading toward artificial intelligence anyway, but did they have to kill my mom for it?" Teagan wasn't crying, but felt an overwhelming sadness deep in her bones. More for her mother than for herself?

"They thought they were doing something to help women. The project notes mentioned that they wanted women to be able to conceive children without men, so they started working on Project M. It was only when they realized that they needed a human to carry the embryo to term that the idea of letting Taryn die came into play. They didn't think they could tell her what they'd done. It doesn't make sense to me either, but that's what they did. I'm so sorry, Teagan. I didn't want you to go digging in the past, but I had no idea that you'd find something like this." Jayce put their arms around Teagan and held her until they could feel her calming down a little.

"I don't even know what to say, I mean, Miranda is a murderer right? But what do I do now? Do I turn her in? And to whom? Do I pretend that I don't know? And how could Noe have kept this from me all of these years? I don't know, Jayce, I just don't know."

"Most of what you need to know is in the files, Teagan, but I'm not sure that you should read them. Miranda is an old woman now. From what I've read, they destroyed the research, decided the ethical implications of creating a baby from synthetic sperm were too great. It's more than ironic that they didn't think that murdering an actual human was wrong. But scientists have always been willing to sacrifice living beings in the name of progress. I just wish that they'd thought this through before hurting your mom. But, please forgive me for saying this, but if they had, I wouldn't have you." Jayce hugged Teagan a little tighter.

Max floated back in the room and handed Jayce the cold towel. Jayce placed it on Teagan's forehead and eased her back onto the settee's pillow. Max floated near the door, unsure of what to do.

"I guess I'll take a day or two and think about what to do. There's no point in calling her now, I wouldn't even know what to say to her." Teagan took Jayce's hand and gave them a little smile.

"That's my girl. We'll figure it out together," said Jayce.

Teagan looked up at Max and gave him a smile. "It's okay Max, it's not your fault. I know you only wanted to protect me, and I know you tried to protect my mother. There's nothing you could have done to stop them." Even though Max had kept the truth from her, she knew that there was no malice in him; he was only doing what he was programmed to do, protect his human.

Max gave Teagan a slight smile, bowed his head, and floated back out of the door.

***

Miranda Li received a notification when Max's files were accessed, and while she had hoped it would never come to this, she had been preparing for this day for a long time. She'd destroyed every bit of evidence associated with Project M and lay on her bed waiting for the injectable to take effect. When she took her last breath, there'd be nothing left of Project M but Teagan, and the few notes in Max's files. She closed her eyes and drifted off, knowing that she and Noe had accomplished what no one else on earth had, and they'd also paid the ultimate price for it.

GLOSSARY/SUGGESTIONS

Author's Note: I'd strongly advise against you trying any of these at home. The following are merely explanations or suggestions of how some humans might find themselves dispatched.

Consummation, or the threat thereof: The act of being consumed (eaten); in this case, by a reptilian alien life form.

Exsanguination: To bleed to death; in one case, induced through Caesarean section, performed by a sneaky spouse and her scientist sidekick best friend. Or in another case, after partial sanguinal consummation (see below) by a fantastical immortal being.

Gunshot: Presumably exsanguination (see above), leading to multiple system failure and cardiac arrest. In both cases, the skullduggery was set in motion by an aggrieved spouse.

Natural causes: Complications related to cancer. In all likelihood, the dispatched's condition was aggravated and exacerbated by her guilty conscious, a direct result of her participation in the plot to murder her wife.

Respiratory failure: Begat by accidental cyanide poisoning, emanating from the machinations of a monomaniacal cat.

Reverse Transmogrification by proxy: The act of transmogrifying into a freakish version of your deepest desire; in this case, abetted by mobile phone application.

Trampling: To be run over; for example, by a large motorized scooter, trying to make its escape from Earth.

Transmogrification: To change in appearance or form, usually into something grotesque or horrifying; conceivably wondrous. For example, into a mythical silver-haired. beast. Or into a person who can transmute what she sees into being.

ACKNOWLEDGEMENTS

To everyone who read and offered comments on these stories, thank you. A special shout out to Krystal A. Smith, who encouraged me to write more speculative fiction, and who always laughs at my silly jokes. To Andrea and Angela, (who finally liked something I wrote!), thank you for your support. Jay, you have been a balm in these trying times, thank you for being you. And finally, to Mango, whose bout with kitty asthma inspired one of the stories in this collection.

CPSIA information can be obtained
at www.ICGtesting.com
Printed in the USA
LVHW092148250321
682535LV00021B/486